CHRISTMAS MOONLIGHT MELODIES

By

Christine L. Henderson

Moonlight, music, and love,

fills a heart with joy!

I appreciate the time you spent reading this story and hope you liked it as much as I enjoyed creating these characters and storyline. I would be especially grateful if you would consider leaving a review of it wherever you purchase your books. Thank you.

Chapter 1

Nicole 'Nikki K" McClellan glanced out at the darkness below her as the plane made the approach to Lehigh Valley International Airport in Pennsylvania. Coming home was the last thing she had planned for this Christmas.

But this time her options were limited. She tossed down the last of the gin and tonic and dropped the three empty mini gin bottles in her glass. Only small bursts of streetlights and businesses were visible below. This was a far cry from the 24/7 lights and late night parties which epitomized Las Vegas, where she had just left.

Vegas was the place to be if you partied into the wee hours of the morning with friends as she'd often done with the band. Only this time her bandmates and all their roadies had each gone their separate ways. The last week with the band was fraught with anger, frustration, and disagreements. Neil Lockwood, the leader of the band, Lockwood & Sutton, checked himself into drug rehab, again, leaving the other band members in the lurch as to what to do next.

Having no other friends in Vegas, her next move was going home. Touring with the band for the last few years and jumping from town to town with no connections other than the band members had left a toll on her mental and physical well-being. Maybe being home again would revitalize her.

After collecting her extra luggage from baggage claim, that represented everything she had left home with when she went on the road, she lugged them to her rental car. She shivered as she pulled up the collar on her short sleek leather jacket and wished it were a furry lined longer one for a bit more warmth. Never had a need for a heavy coat when the band had gigs. It was just a short run from their custom RV to a dressing room or the stage. Once she was home she'd borrow one of her mom's parkas to keep warm and add some gloves as well.

Though it had only been a short walk from the heated car rental storefront, where she picked up her key fob, her hands already felt like they were frozen. Jumping into the car and turning on the ignition she waited impatiently for the heat to come on. Blowing on her hands and rubbing them together she gazed through the windshield.

A flurry of delicate snowflakes shimmered in the glow of the parking lot lights. Seeing them brought blissful memories of nighttime skiing in the Poconos with friends. Some of them had never left her hometown, including Kayla, her best friend. Spending time together again shopping and even skiing would be fun.

Perhaps Michael would be there as well. She let out a deep sigh as tears welled in her eyes. *How many times did I start calls or texts but stopped? I wanted to reach out to him, but I couldn't for the hurt I caused by choosing my fame over our love.* Though they weren't in contact, that didn't stop her from following his career. She knew the songs he penned for others that became hits. And then his own rise to stardom with his band Gone South.

But he dropped out of the limelight. He was a big enough name that she would have read something in the news if he been in a terrible accident or died of a drug overdose. He could have returned home, but she'd been afraid to ask Kayla what she might have heard about Michael. If he were married and had a family, it would cut like a knife to her heart. It had been seven years since she left, but she never stopped loving him.

Maybe they could start fresh again like the stories told in the popular country music songs. As she made her way to the highway, she hoped for a spark of Christmas magic that could bring back a love to keep her warm or would she stay as cold as ice like she felt at this moment.

Nikki stopped to get an energy drink to keep her alert before she hit the Interstate and county roads that were black and barren. Since it was the weekend after Thanksgiving, the local radio station was playing only Christmas songs.

When Elvis Presley's "Blue Christmas," came on, she smacked the dashboard. "Hope you're feeling blue now, Neil, trying to get your life back together again. I was so starry eyed and naïve when you offered me a spot in the band. I thought you cared for me. We'd be the most popular celebrity couple in magazines and on TV entertainment news. But it was only make believe. I was only your newest playmate. One of a never-ending line of starstruck females."

Her phone ringing tone interrupted her ranting. The caller ID showed it was her mom.

"Hi Mom, already on the road. Maybe 30 minutes into the drive. Sorry I forgot to call."

"Are you tired? Do you want me to stay on the phone and talk?"

"No, Mom. Not necessary. Get some sleep. I know Saturdays can be long days at the inn for you. I still have a key to our family apartment there. No need to wait up for me."

"That's sweet of you. I'm exhausted and would like to feel rested in the morning for church."

"You're going to church?" Nikki sputtered. "It's not even Christmas. Is tomorrow some kind of special event for the town?"

"No, just a normal Sunday. I go to Abundant Life Church on a regular basis."

"Since when?" Growing up, church attendance was only at Christmas, Easter and the occasional wedding. Otherwise, her parents were always too busy running their resort inn.

"I guess it goes back to when your dad died. Everyone was so nice in helping me through my grieving process. They showed me what God's love is all about. I wanted more of that. I started going from time to time. Now it's a big part of my life."

Thinking back to her dad's funeral, Nikki's heart ached. A twinge of guilt hit her for not calling more often before he died nor since to check more regularly on her mom. Most of the planning for the memorial service was a blur. It was her first experience in dealing the death of someone near to her. She was an emotional wreck. Her mom had chosen Abundant Life church because it was large enough to hold all the people who knew her dad and wanted to pay their respects.

Nikki tapped her fingers on the steering wheel. "You're not expecting me to go to church with you, are you? I could really use the sleep once I get in."

"No, Nicole. You're free to make your own decisions. Just wanted to let you know I'll be back around noon. I've got someone who covers for me at the inn for the morning shift. Sleep as long as you like. The inn's breakfast service ends at 10:00. Do whatever suits you. Tonight I made the gingerbread cookies you like. I'll leave them covered on the counter in case you want a snack when you get home. I'm so glad you're going to be here for a while. We'll have such a wonderful Christmas together."

"I hate to say it Mom, but I think Neil's breakdown came at the right time. I sure need some down time myself."

"Well, honey, God works in mysterious ways. And I think coming home was part of his plan. Now drive safely, and I'll see you tomorrow. Love you."

"Love you back." Nikki smiled as she disconnected the call. When she was a kid the kickoff to their holiday baking was always gingerbread cookies. *Glad to know that's a tradition Mom wants to continue. What will I do for the next 30 days while Neil's in rehab? And then what? We only have one gig temporarily scheduled for the end of January. Will we still be a band?*

Chapter 2

Nikki woke feeling groggy around 11:00 AM. Throwing her legs over the side of the bed, she scanned the time warp that was her bedroom. Nothing had changed since she'd left seven years ago. Framed photos of her appearances on the TV talent show dotted the shelves on one wall and posters of the musicals where she played the lead with Michael in high school adorned another wall.

She traipsed over to the "Dreamland" poster and let her fingers dance across the letters as a pang of sorrow gripped her for the intervening years she had missed with Michael. *Why did I let fame override our plans for the future? He was my world, but I gave up on us. Can I bear seeing him again? What will*

I do if he rejects me like I did to him way back then?

Trudging into the hall bathroom, she splashed water on her face and combed her hair. Then, she threw on the same clothes from last night, picked up her phone, and headed down the hall to the staircase that would take her the to the inn's kitchen. Hopefully there would be something interesting left over from the breakfast buffet.

As she walked, she tapped in Kayla's number, but the call went to voicemail. The website for the coffee shop Kayla ran showed it wouldn't open till noon on Sundays. Nothing appealed to her in the refrigerator, so she'd make do with some of her Mom's signature spiced tea and her gingerbread cookies.

After she showered and perused her old closet for a sweater, boots, jeans, and a coat much thicker than what she wore last night she felt ready to leave. Driving through downtown, she smiled seeing some of the long established shops she'd loved in her teen years were still there.

Few people were out shopping yet, so she was able to find a parking space steps away from the Kayla's shop. The Coffee Haven & Sweets sign was encircled with Christmas lights and faux candy canes. This was their favorite hangout as teens and they even worked there part-time in the summer. Back then it had been owned by Marge and John Trainor, who were better known as Mom and Pop T. After high school, Kayla continued to work there as she took business courses at the local community college.

When Mom and Pop T started to make plans to retire, they worked out a business agreement with Kayla so she could buy the shop. They knew she loved it as much as they had, and it would continue to exist in caring hands.

Nikki quickly stepped inside and closed the door to keep out the chilling breeze rolling down the street. Getting out of the cold and smelling the tantalizing scent of freshly baked pastries awakened her appetite. That's one of the main things that hadn't changed in the shop. There was still a dazzling display of pastries and trays of assorted chocolate delights. Kayla had also added a showcase of gift display boxes from her store and some of the other local merchants for added sales.

A high-pitched squeal punctured the air. "I can't believe you're here," Kayla said as she ran to her friend and wrapped her in a hug. "When did you get in?"

"Late last night. Got a rental car so I'll have my own wheels to come and go as I please."

Kayla put her arm around Nikki's shoulder and began singing, "You are my shining star. Yes, you are. Yes, you are."

Nikki shook her head and gritted her teeth behind a smile. That's what Neil called her until someone else caught his fancy. Though she didn't come in as number one on "America's Best New Talent," she was starstruck by Neil when he signed her on with the band.

Everything about being part of the band was exhilarating at first. When her relationship with Neil fizzled, she didn't leave the band because she loved the adrenaline rush of being on stage and seeing all the fans. But her once hopeful dream of having the fans hear more of her singing solos or duos with Neil had faded. The solos and duets were few and far between.

However, she did get her share of royalties and upgraded pay for being a regular in the band. That is if they had gigs which were lacking at the moment. A reminder that she needed to be cautious with her spending for the time being until she knew there would be continued gigs.

"You know, I really wish you wouldn't call me a star," Nikki sighed. "I'm one of the singers, not the lead singer. Besides, the band is on hiatus with Neil in drug rehab for the next 30 days. As of now, our tour plans are on hold." Nikki held up her hands showing air quotes. "So, my 'shining star' is quickly fading."

"Being part of a major band is a star by my standards, even if you're on hiatus." Kayla walked back behind the counter and pointed to the wall. "I still believe one of these days I'm gonna have your picture up there showing you grinning ear to ear holding your first Grammy with me by your side. Your autograph will read, 'I owe all my fame to my best friend, Kayla.' Just own it. You're a celebrity."

When Kayla pointed to the wall, Nikki noticed a diamond ring on her hand shimmering under the lights. "What's with the ring?"

"You took long enough to notice." Kayla giddily held her left hand in front of Nikki.

"Who's the lucky guy?" Nikki reached over the counter and gave her friend a hug.

Kayla gazed at the ring and smiled. "His name is Luke Fletcher. He's not anyone from the old days. He moved here two years ago. I never thought he'd be the one. Love has a way of surprising you that way. We clicked right away when we met. He made me laugh with his puns. We worked on some committees together and became friends. Soon we began thinking it could be something more."

"Are the two of you living together now?"

"Heavens no. I don't think that would work well with his job." Kayla laughed. "He's the associate pastor at Abundant Life Church."

Nikki's eyes bugged out. "You're marrying a pastor? I didn't know you were into church that much."

"I don't know why that would seem like a surprise. I sang in the church choir while we were in high school, and I still sing in the choir at church." Kayla poured a cup of coffee for herself.

"Yeah, I seem to recall some Christmas concerts in a church. Never thought it was something you'd keep doing."

"Really? I've love singing like you do and praising God in church is special."

The chimes over the front door jingled announcing a customer had walked in as Nikki gave her friend a high-five. "Sounds like that's a match made in heaven."

"I like the sound of a match made in heaven. Could be a great song title."

Nikki's heart raced. She had never forgotten that deep resonant voice that filled her heart with joy and the man who once held her close and whispered that their love would last forever -- Michael. She sat frozen, unable to move and had to remember to breathe.

"How long are you in town, Nicole?" Michael asked as he stepped closer.

Nikki took in a breath and swiveled her stool around to face him. He was now only steps away. She sat transfixed as if she were a mannequin. Her gaze locked onto his deep piercing blue eyes that seemed to be seeking out every thought she had. His black hair was short now, but it still had that over-one-eye dip that made her want to reach up and run her fingers through it. His towering six-foot frame remained as remarkably fit as ever, making her wish she could slip against his chest and let him wrap her in his embrace. But she'd lost that right when she walked out on him to take the gig with Lockwood & Sutton.

"Through…the holidays," she stuttered, tugging at her hair. "How about you?"

"Michael lives here. I thought you knew that. He's the music director at Abundant Life Church. And what a blessing he is."

"So that's what happened to you after you disbanded your band, Gone South. *Funny, Mom didn't mention that.*

"You followed my career?" Michael's trademark smile curved up to one side with one eyebrow raised.

Nikki felt the heat of a blush rise up her face as her hand fluttered in the air. "It would be hard not to. Gone South was a hot band. You had a string of top ten hits. And your songwriting skills provided great songs for other singers as well."

She held a tight smile so her lips wouldn't quiver. Michael had wanted her to be in his band, but he hadn't yet risen to fame like Lockwood & Sutton. Rather than waiting for his star to shine, she ran to the already famous group, only leaving a text message saying. "Got my big break. Going on tour. Best of luck with the band."

"What can I get you to drink, Michael? Will it be your usual black coffee with a touch of cinnamon?"

Michael nodded and slipped onto the stool next to Nikki as if it were something he had never stopped doing all the time. In reaction to his move, Nikki began rubbing her hands up and down her thighs wishing she had a gin and tonic in her hands to calm her nerves.

"How about you, Nikki? Want your regular chai latte without the cinnamon garnish? Maybe you could change it up and try a coffee for once?"

Nikki scrunched up her nose. "I'm sure you make a mean cup of coffee, but it's still not what I like to drink."

That response brought laughs from both Kayla and Michael, which helped Nikki relax.

While Kayla brewed their beverages, she added, "Michael is still creating music. He's in rehearsals now for the church's Christmas concert."

"True. My musical cast now comprises of teenagers and adults," Michael added. "Little kids will be in the program as well, but our youth minister is managing them.

As Kayla handed over the beverages to the two of them she added, "You should go to one of their rehearsals. It will bring back memories of our high school musicals, except Michael is more appealing to the eyes than our music director was. That causes many flirtatious glances at him from the singers, but Michael keeps it all professional."

Nikki watched as Michael blushed at Kayla's comments. *Kayla didn't mention a girlfriend. There's no ring on his finger, so he could be single. Why should I care or even notice? I lost my chance for our relationship years ago. Besides, I'm only here temporarily.* She cupped her hands around her mug of tea, sniffed its aromatic scent, and licked a dab of the whipped cream, before taking a sip. "Ah, now that's what I like."

Michael lifted his coffee up in a toast. "Here's to a wonderful Christmas season."

Nikki raised her mug to his and once again became lost in his eyes. Her heart pounded so wildly she thought he might hear it. To break away from staring, Nikki pulled off her large multi-colored wool cap, and then fluffed up her hair.

Kayla's mouth dropped open at seeing the purple and red streaks that colored Nikki's hair. "Wow, I thought that hair color was just a wig. I never imagined it was your real hair."

Nikki rolled her eyes. "Yeah, I guess it's a bit weird for Culver Creek. I should buy some hair dye today to get it back to something more normal."

"Yeah, blend in, unless you want people to notice you, ask for your autograph, or take selfies with you," Kayla replied.

"No, no, no." Nikki held up a hand in protest. "Blending in is what I want. I don't want to answer questions about the band."

Michael grinned. "I know what that's like. I got tired of answering the same question about why I left the band. I had a lot of things to work out in my head, and I wanted to be left alone."

"Do you want to be left alone, Nikki?" Kayla asked as she leaned on the counter.

Nikki almost spit out her tea on hearing Kayla's teasing remark. "Umm, not at all. I came back to visit with old friends."

"Great! How about dinner out on Tuesday? It's my day off. Not everyone moved away like you. Would that work for you as well, Michael?"

Michael gave her a thumbs up and Nikki nodded.

"I'll make the calls to Bella, Todd, Ginny, and Ray," Kayla added. "I'll make reservations for 6:00 pm at Sal's."

Michael stood and left money on the counter for his coffee. "Gotta run. Have a jam session with some friends. See you both Tuesday."

As he turned and walked away, Nikki's eyes followed him, and her heart sank. She turned back to her tea and sighed.

"Hard seeing him again, isn't it? The way you looked at him seems like you still have feelings for him."

Nikki shrugged and stared into her tea. "How would that be possible? We split a long time ago."

"Some feelings never die. And I think he's still in love with you."

Nikki's head bolted up. "You do?"

"Yup. But I think some healing still needs to be done. Are you willing to work through that?"

Nikki sipped her tea. "Do you know that at one time he asked me to be part of his band?"

"What? You would have been great together."

"I told him no. I had one year left to finish my music degree. Then I entered 'America's Best New Talent' and got the job with Lockwood & Sutton and nothing else mattered."

"Wow. you never told me what broke the two of you apart."

"I slammed the door on our relationship. I was so blind back then. Music and fame were my only focus. Everything else took second place."

"So you both got the fame you were looking for."

"But he's not in a band anymore. He's a church music director. How did that happen?"

"Seems he had some sort of spiritual awakening when he was on the road and turned to Jesus. His calling now is bringing people closer to God through his music. Since you're here for Christmas, maybe you could get a spot in his show?"

Nikki rolled her eyes and laughed. "Haven't been in church in years. It might burn up if I passed through the doors."

Kayla chuckled and shook her head. "You're always welcome in church. Chat with him about it Tuesday. I still remember what great stars you both were in our high school musicals."

"I'll think about it. How about warming up one of your fresh cranberry orange scones for me?"

"Coming right up."

Nikki folded her hands under her chin. *Me singing in a quiet church choir? That's a laugh. But it would give me more time with him. Music did bring us together. Could it bring us back together again? Or is that too much of a long shot to hope for?*

Chapter 3

Michael set in his raised chair facing his teen choir as they fidgeted and rehearsed "O Holy Night" for the Christmas program. The group was slowly forming a cohesive sound as they became comfortable with each other, but he still hadn't chosen someone to sing the solo part for that song. No one who auditioned fulfilled what he had envisioned.

He continued to hold auditions and hoped God would send him the right person for the part. His current group of singers may have lacked professional training, but they more than made up for that with their enthusiasm for singing and praising God.

His mind drifted back to the auditions he'd done in high school. He was always surprised when he scored the male leads, and doing duets with Nicole was pure joy. Those times were wonderful, and he thought they'd continue singing together after high school. But dreams don't always come true. The love of music brought them together and also tore them apart.

He followed her career with Lockwood and Sutton and even attended one of their concerts when he had some free time during one of his band's tours. He saw the enthusiasm she had for singing in the band and was happy she was living her musical dream, but it hurt that it hadn't been with him.

Letting his reverie slip away, his attention returned to his choir. He gave out music sheets for two more songs they'd be performing in the show. "Thanks for all the hard work you're doing. Let's work on this new music. I'm ready for a couple more hours if…"

His momentary hesitation brought forth a spontaneous groan that worked through the singers and made him laugh.

"Don't worry, I'm not going to ask you to do that. I can see you would rather be outside enjoying the snow. So, go. Just promise you'll practice the songs at home before the next rehearsal."

While Michael was dismissing everyone, Luke Fletcher, the associate pastor, came into the choir room and sat quietly in one of the front chairs waiting to talk to Michael. It took a few minutes for everyone to pick up their coats and books and say their goodbyes to each other and greet the pastor before leaving.

When they were alone, Michael came and sat beside Luke. "What brings you to one of my rehearsals?"

"Curious to see how everything is coming along and to ask you a question."

Michael leaned back and put his hands behind his head. "It's a lot more complicated than when I was in one of these as a teenager. Always wish we had more volunteers, but we'll still do well. What's your other question?"

"Kayla told me we're having dinner together tomorrow night to celebrate the return of an old friend named Nikki or Nicole. Not sure what she goes by. Is she someone you knew well?"

Michael looked up at the stage, but his focus wasn't there. "Sure did. We played the romantic leads in our high school musicals. We both had dreams of becoming famous singers. During high school I started a band that eventually got regular gigs and moved on to being the opening act for bigger name bands. I asked her to be one of our backup singers, but she refused. At that point, she was finishing her music degree. Then she entered a TV competition, and everything changed. She signed on to a big-name band and was gone in a flash. Nothing else mattered to her but her stardom."

"Did you ever tour together?"

"Not at all. Her band, Lockwood & Sutton, is a mix of R&B and rock with a British flair. We were southern rock. Our band's name was Gone South. It took us two more years and a second album that went platinum to be able to draw a crowd to fill an arena like they did. My songwriting at that time didn't exactly glorify God, but several of my songs were picked up by other singers. I get royalties, not mega ones, but it's still a treat when the money drops into my account."

"What was being a headliner like?"

'Wow." Michael rang his fingers through his hair and blew out a deep breath. "It was mind blowing. But being at the top of our game really messed with our heads. Being celebrities, we began to think we could do whatever we wanted and indulge in whatever pleased us at the moment. I regret to say there were nights I woke up in bed with someone whose name I didn't even know. Drugs and alcohol after the shows kept everything in a haze. Praise God, I was delivered from that."

"How?"

"One evening after an argument with a band member, I went for a walk to clear my head. Stopped by a coffee shop where I heard someone playing guitar. I love listening to live music, so I went inside. The place was packed. Everyone was singing along with him. The songs told of love and forgiveness, how God always gives us second chances, and how he reaches out to us."

Luke nodded in understanding. "God was reaching out to you."

"Yes, he was. The songs resonated with me. I stayed till he finished his final set. It brought back memories of singing with Nicole and other friends from school. There wasn't a radical change in me that night, but God was working in me. I began listening to Christian music. When I heard Kris Kristofferson's song, 'Why Me Lord,' I felt those words were aimed straight at my heart. I knew it was time to break away from that lifestyle and get back in line with a life that God wanted for me." Michael scrolled through his phone's pictures and opened the folder showing images of his last days with his band to show Luke.

"Whoa! Long hair and a full beard. I would never recognize you from those pictures."

Michael smirked. "And I'd bet my old band members wouldn't recognize me today either. That was three and a half years ago. My life has really turned around. I came home and started at Abundant Life as an assistant youth leader and worked on my degree in my spare time. Through hard work and a devotion to God, I was selected as the music ministry director when the position came open. That was right before you came here."

"Sounds like the two of you have some catching up to do. I know you're tired. Finish whatever you have to do. I'll see you tomorrow."

Michael leaned back in his chair and closed his eyes for a minute. Seeing Nicole again was a real gut punch. He thought he was over her. But those old feelings came rushing back. *Well, Nikki, are you just passing through again? Or has God given us a second chance at love?*

Chapter 4

Nikki stared at the mirror taking in her new appearance. Gone were the streaks of red and purple. Her hair now showed a rich chestnut color that gave a glow to her skin tone. She wore new chocolate colored corduroy pants and a scoop neck hunter green sweater with small gold balls and red glass beads around the neckline. For a final touch, she added earrings with a trio of dangling snowflakes to complete the Christmas look. She nodded approval for the image she saw in the mirror -- classy but casual. Definitely not rock star glam.

She gritted her teeth and frowned. *No, this isn't right. I've gotta find something else.*

Turning to go back into the closet for the third time, she stopped in mid step and stomped her foot. *No, this is fine. Why am I so nervous about how I look? This isn't an interview or a photo shoot, It's just dinner and drinks with friends... But one of those friends is Michael.*

Nikki blew out a deep breath, then headed for the small kitchen in the apartment. *What I need is a drink to calm my nerves.* She poured herself a glass of red wine, finished it, then refilled the glass to the rim, and tossed the empty bottle in the trash. She gulped down the first swig from the second glass and quickly downed the rest of it. Opening her purse, found a mint, popped it in her mouth, then picked up her wool coat and left the room.

When she walked into the living room, her mom had just entered their apartment. "My word, Nicole, don't you look wonderful. I love what you've done to your hair. That color suits you. It looks like you were born with it."

"You really like it?"

"Yes. And I love the Christmassy look of your clothes." Mom gave her a hug. "Now scoot out of here. Have a fun evening with your friends."

Nikki kissed her mom on the cheek and said goodbye before heading out the door. The sooner she got there the better. Another drink would calm the butterflies fluttering around her stomach and crashing into each other.

Just as Nikki turned on the car's ignition, her cell phone buzzed. The ring tone let her know it was from one of her band members. "Hey. Jasper. What's going on? What's all the noise in the background?"

"Nikki, babe. Good to hear your voice. Wish you were here. We're at an after party from the concert we just played in London."

"What concert?"

"After Neil went off to his rehab place, I didn't want to go stir crazy and end up joining him there. Made some calls to my mates here in London. Seems one of the singers in

'Rhythmicity' got herself pregnant and has that morning sickness thing. Macie's a good replacement and they wanted me on bass as well. Such a rush being back here again. Why don't you come join us?"

"Jasper, I just got home. I haven't visited my mom in three years. I can't just up and leave."

" Yeah, I understand the family thing. Me mum likes that I'll be here for Christmas. But do at least come for New Year's Eve. The band's got a gig at South Bank Center. It's the biggest event in London. It'll be a blast. We'd love to have you here to add to the mix. I'll get them to buy you a first-class ticket and your own hotel room."

By the time Jasper said the last several words, the background noise of people and music was overwhelming. She cupped her hand over the phone to make her voice as clear as possible. "What about Neil? Isn't his rehab release the twenty-eighth?"

"Nikki, babe, you know we can't really count on Neil. This is his third rehab this year. For now, my plans with this band are only through New Year's Eve. If Neil's up to it, he'd be welcome, too. Seriously, think about coming over. I'll check back with you next week. Kiss. Kiss. Bye now."

Nikki clicked off and sat in silence. It had been a few years since the band had played there. She remembered what a thrill it was for them being in their hometown. That gig was a total rush, and it was one of the few times she felt like a mega star being with them.

Doing that event would feel pretty great. But seeing how excited her mom was about having her home for the holidays and then up and leaving so quickly would break her heart. And Neil's rehab results could be temporary *again*. It was all too much to think about. She wasn't sure what to do. No real need to decide now. Tonight, she had plans with her friends and was now running late.

Chapter 5

When Nikki arrived at Sal's Pizzeria it looked pretty much the same, except for a larger and more modern sign. The parking lot was mostly full. Hopefully, Kayla had reserved a table, or it would be a long wait. Nikki looked in the car's mirror to make sure there weren't any smudges on her makeup. She threw a couple of small breath mints in her mouth, then got out of the car.

Twinkling lights around the restaurant's covered entrance gave it a festive appeal. Looking up, she laughed at the big Santa on the roof holding a gigantic pizza box in his hands.

That Christmas decoration hadn't changed though it looked more weathered.

While the exterior of the building had only minor changes, the interior was dramatically different. Gone were the bright red booths and checkered plastic tablecloths. Now mahogany colored wood chairs and tabletops with a granite finish were in place. The peeling travel posters of Italy had disappeared and replaced with soft murals of vineyards and rolling landscapes of Italy.

Glancing at the tables, she could see they finally got their full liquor license as beer, wine, and cocktail glasses were in evidence. She hoped they had a good wine list because she was ready for another glass. As her gaze swept the room, she noticed Kayla waving at her.

Everyone Kayla had mentioned was there, including Michael. Seeing him made her pulse race into overdrive. *How could he still do that after all these years? I can't start daydreaming of a life together. I'm only going to be here a few weeks. And I burned that bridge to a reconciliation when I left.*

Scanning the table where her friends sat she noted the only empty chair was the one at the corner of the table with Kayla on one side and Michael across from her. No doubt that was Kayla's doing. "Hi all. Sorry for being late." Nikki held up her hands in an air of appeasement. "I can assure you it's not a diva thing. I wouldn't do that to old friends. But as I was leaving, I got a call from one of my bandmates who just finished a show in London, and he wanted to tell me all about it."

This statement elicited looks of surprise from those around the table. Kayla was the first to blurt out a comment. "Your band is in London? You didn't tell me you quit the band. Or did something else happen?"

Nikki's mouth fell open. "I didn't leave the band, nor did they fire me. While our band is on a break, a couple of the band members joined with friends in another band for a show. We'll probably get back together again after the holidays. This is just a temporary break. At least that's the plan for now."

"That's great," Kayla added. "That means you'll still be able to celebrate the holidays with us. So, let's raise a toast..."

The only glass near Nikki was the water glass, so she raised it, while looking about for a server who could get her a drink.

As everyone raised their glasses, Kayla continued. "To old friends and the memories we share. To the joy of Christmas together again. And to a future we hope to be bright."

"To friends" came the response from those around the table.

Kayla waved over their server. "While Nikki takes a few minutes to review the menu, let's start giving our orders. I'll begin."

When it was Nikki's turn, she gave her food order, then asked the server to bring a glass of one of their mid-priced red wines. It mattered little to her that all the others at the table had ordered only sodas, iced tea, or coffee. She needed a glass of wine, and the server quickly delivered it.

Several conversations bubbled around the table, giving Nikki time to drink her wine. She was comfortable with just listening and trying to catch up with what was happening in their lives. That is until Bella directed a question to her.

"So, Nicole, or do you prefer Nikki? What's it feel like being back home after playing those big concert venues?"

"Nikki or Nicole, either is fine to me. Waking up in the same town for the next six weeks is a big change. Usually, we're on the road going from town to town. I'm looking forward to celebrating Christmas at home this year."

"Do you get nervous when you're on stage?" asked Bella.

Nikki shrugged. "When I first step on that stage and see a ton of people who will be watching my every move, I worry I'll mess up the lyrics. You don't get do-overs when you're live. When you were a cheerleader, Bella, I bet having everybody watch what you were doing made you nervous, too." After finishing her statement, she finished her wine and waved the server over for another.

"Oh yeah, I definitely got the jitters," Bella replied." "Thank God, we practiced a lot to get it perfect."

As Bella finished her statement, two servers arrived and delivered the food. Once everyone had their meals, Kayla said, "Luke would you say the prayer, please."

Confused, Nikki watched as everyone bowed their heads and reached out their hands to one another. Awkwardly, she joined in, not knowing what to expect. She never said a prayer before a meal and certainly wouldn't have considered praying in a restaurant, but her friends seemed comfortable with the action. Luke's words were heartfelt and thankfully they were short. Then everyone added, "Amen," and began to eat.

The only sounds from the table for the next few minutes were of utensils tapping on plates as each enjoyed their dinner. Then Nikki asked. "What about you, Luke? Do you get nervous in front of everyone when you give one of your talks in church?"

Luke grinned. "Not nearly as much as I did when I decided to ask Kayla to marry me."

This elicited laughter around the table and then Luke continued. "I rehearsed them over and over until I knew them by heart. I still spend a lot of time on study, research, and prayer. And I remind myself it's not about me, but Jesus, and I ask for the Holy Spirit's inspiration."

While Luke was speaking, Nikki cast a glance at Bella who was leaning against Ray's shoulder. *Funny how things change after high school. Back then, Ray wasn't even on Bella's radar. Todd and Ginny were at different ends of the spectrum. He was a geek and she was always drawing something in one of her sketch pads. But somehow they discovered something in common. And everyone thought it was a no-brainer that Michael and I would live happily ever after.* She finished her wine and ordered another.

The conversation then turned to updates on other people from high school. Some had left town and made a name for themselves in the corporate world, but Nikki smugly thought none could claim as famous a career as hers.

Then she turned to Michael. *Why does he look so confident and self-assured? He was the one who left the music business. Could he not cut it, so he ran from it? I'm the one still playing for the mega crowds and should feel like I'm on top of the world, but I don't feel how he looks. It's not fair.*

She motioned for the server to bring another glass of wine, then turned to Michael "What's it like being stuck at a church after playing to thousands of screaming fans? Couldn't cut it? Now you're directing Christmas music for hundreds at your church. How's that working out for you?"

Nikki flinched hearing how mockingly those words came out of her mouth. *OMG. I was just thinking that. I didn't mean to say it.* She cleared her throat and quickly added, "It must bring you a lot of joy, right?" Nikki watched Michael's eyes cloud over for a moment with sadness before quickly turning to a look of compassion.

Michael shrugged. "Sure, playing to huge crowds was ego inflating along with topping the music charts. I've always loved writing music that touches people's hearts. That hasn't changed. Only now I create music to glorify and honor God. I certainly don't miss the nonstop touring. Being on the road so much can really wear you down. Wouldn't you agree Nikki?"

Nikki wanted to say I'm sorry, but instead merely nodded and smiled. Michael's response to her snippy question was gentle and heartfelt. "Yes, the fans are wonderful, but the travel is draining. Bet none of you have traveled as much as I have."

There was silence and a chill around the table, until Kayla added, "The town's Christmas food and craft fair is next week. Who has suggestions for what I should make for my booth?"

The others quickly threw out ideas, except for Nikki. She listened as the conversation went from one topic to another and occasionally dropped a snide remark when she thought they were ignoring her. Tiring of the banter she called for her bill and got up to leave.

When Nikki rose from the table, Kayla nudged Luke for the two of them to do the same. Luke paid their bill, while Kayla caught up with Nikki and grabbed her arm before she reached the door. "Nikki, give me your car key. You're in no condition to drive. I'm taking you home and Luke will follow behind in his car." Nikki glared at her friend knowing she wouldn't relent on her request. She handed over her key. "Here you go Missy Too Good. What I had tonight is nothing compared to the alcohol and drugs I've had with the band." Without waiting for a reply, she walked out the door with Kayla and Luke not far behind.

Chapter 6

Kayla was still upset about needing to drive Nikki home when she called to check on her the next morning. It took several rings before Nikki finally picked up the call. As soon as she did, Kayla snapped. "What in the world got into you last night?"

"What do you mean? It's all a bit hazy to me right now. My head is pounding and my stomach's not doing much better."

"You don't remember that I had to drive you home?"

"You dropped me off? No, I drove my car last night. You didn't pick me up."

"Yes, you drove the car over to Sal's last night, but you were in no condition to drive home."

"What? All I remember drinking were a few glasses of wine. I've drunk more than that many times when we're on the road without it affecting me."

"Sorry, Nikki. That wasn't the case last night."

"So, where's my car now? I need it today."

"Your car is in the driveway. And your key is in your purse."

"How did you get home then?"

"I came with Luke last night. I drove your car. He followed me to your house."

Kayla sighed. "You really don't remember? It started when you made it sound like Michael was lowering himself to work as a church music minister. You tried to cover that up with a compliment, but you didn't stop there. You made snide remarks to everyone at the table, even Luke. What was that all about? I've never seen you that drunk even as a teenager trying to act grown up."

"You're exaggerating. I don' t remember being snippy," Nikki said defensively.

"Well, you were. That might pass for normal behavior around your band buddies, but it's hurtful here."

"I'm sorry. That's not like me. I can't imagine I'd do that."

"Maybe you need to lay off alcohol for a while, Nikki. Drinking doesn't improve your wit, nor will it clear your thinking about your future, which you said you wanted to do while you were here."

"Okay, maybe I did overdo it a little. Cut me some slack. I just got off the road and don't know how to do normal right now. I promise I'll try to do better. Is there anything else you wanted to talk about?"

"Well, yeah. I may not want to be around you right now, but I need some assistance. You promised you'd help me put together goodie packages for the Senior Center at 2:00 today.

Are you still going to make it?"

Nikki was silent for a moment. All she wanted to do was take something for her pounding headache and lie down. Being cheery and helpful was not her current frame of mind. Kayla sounded really upset and reneging on a promise she made last night wouldn't improve things. Even if she didn't remember it. The alarm clock by her bed showed 11:40. "Sure I can do that. Where are we meeting? At the coffee shop or at your place?"

"My home. Don't have the space to spread out at the shop and still have room for customers. I've got a couple of part-timers covering for me so I can get this done."

"See you soon."

"Right, but do yourself a favor, Nikki. No booze before you come over, okay?"

Nikki's mouth opened and her mind raced to return with a snide remark, but decided this wasn't the time for that. "Don't worry I won't. Bye."

She disconnected the call and threw her phone on the bed. Her nostrils flared and her eyebrows furrowed in a deep vee. *You'd think with our friendship, she'd cut me some slack. Kayla's got to be over exaggerating.*

She stormed into the bathroom but stopped short when she saw her face in the mirror. Her hair looked like she'd been in a horror movie and her makeup was all smudged. *Wow. I must have just crashed into bed. Did that a time or two after a concert when I was exhausted but didn't think I'd do it at home. Maybe Kayla is right. I drank too much. Had a blackout. Can't remember the bad stuff I said. Better have Kayla can fill me in, so I can make things right with the others. I'll pick up something special for her on my way over as my first apology.*

In the shower, she let the warm water wash over her body for several minutes, wishing it could wash away the hangover as well. The shower refreshed her, and light touches of makeup improved her earlier mirror view. Once she threw on a Christmas T-shirt, jeans, and boots, she headed to the inn's kitchen to see what remained of the breakfast for the guests.

Opening the refrigerator, Nikki's gaze zeroed in on a partial quiche, a capped bottle of champagne, and a pitcher of orange juice. She put a wedge of the quiche in the microwave to heat, then poured equal amounts of champagne and orange juice into a glass.

Taking a bottle of ibuprofen out of one of the cabinets, she poured out a couple and popped them into her mouth, then washed them down with her freshly made mimosa. Nikki took another sip enjoying the sweet and tangy taste. For now, she'd just have one, or maybe two at the most. What harm could that do? Had to have a clear head to talk to her friend and gain back her trust.

That started with being on time. Looking at the kitchen clock, it was time to leave. After downing her glass and a few bites of the quiche, she picked up her coat, keys, and purse, then headed out the door.

Chapter 7

Nikki stepped out of her car in the downtown public parking lot and was immediately hit with a gust of snowflakes that ruffled her hair. *Hope I can get the shopping done before I'm totally frozen. Not used to this chilly weather anymore. Wonder where I can get a mug of hot mulled wine to take off the chill?*

She pulled up her coat collar and walked down Market Street, alternating between looking at store windows and scrolling through her phone for Christmas gift ideas for Kayla.

When she stopped to look at a nearby store window display, she saw Michael was just a few feet in front of her. She froze in her steps and pretended to be vastly interested in what the store was promoting, but not before Michael caught her eye and called out her name. There was no way she could pretend she didn't see him now. Her face felt flushed even with the wind whipping down the street.

"Hi, umm, it's good to see you again, Michael. "About last night…" She was at a loss for words. Her mind was mush. Kayla told her she had said a number of nasty things to Michael but didn't elaborate.. She needed to apologize, but she couldn't remember what she had said. "I apparently said some things to you that were out of line –"

Michael crossed his arms over his chest and narrowed his eyes. "You *apparently* said something. Don't you recall what you said last night?"

Nicki bit her lip and shrugged. "Last night is a bit sketchy to me."

He shook his head and let out a deep breath. His eyes bore into hers as he spoke. "Let me refresh your memory. You said I couldn't cut it in the real music world, so I slunk into playing music at a church. That I was acting superior about playing music for God and it was such a joke."

Nikki's eyes bugged out and her mouth dropped open. "No, I wouldn't have said that. You're making a horrible joke."

"Unfortunately, I'm not. And I'm not the only one you attacked. What you said hurt me and the others at the table. I didn't leave the country music scene because I couldn't cut it. It was because I saw how it was wrecking my life. I saw what the drugs, alcohol, and fame we're doing to me. I didn't want to become one of those celebrity front page headlines who was found dead in a hotel room due to an overdose or choking on my own vomit. I wanted my life to be worth more than that. Surprisingly, what made a difference was stepping into a coffee shop where a guy was singing his heart out about Jesus. That got my attention.

I knew I had to quit the band if I wanted to get my life back on the right track. I started going to AA and NA meetings and joined a men's prayer group. I kept writing songs but my focus changed. You may find it hard to believe at this point, but I get more fulfillment from my music career now than I did when I was in the band. So what you said last night was very upsetting."

Nikki shoulders slumped. "It's hard for me to believe I could have said those things. I'm not spiteful like that. Guess my thoughts got a bit jumbled up from what I was thinking randomly, my frustrations with my band, and I blurted out those…um words… without thinking what I was saying."

Michael gave her a quizzical look, then brought a finger to his lips. "You don't remember anything about last night…do you?"

Nikki squeezed her eyes shut and whispered. "I remember being excited about coming to the restaurant and seeing you again." "And that's it?" Nikki nodded.

Michael shook his head, then rested his hands on her shoulders. "You don't remember because you were in a blackout. Had a few drinks before you came to the restaurant? Right? Probably had a couple this morning?"

"So, what if I did?" Nikki's pushed him away and her forehead creased in heavy lines as she glared at him.

"You've got a drinking problem, maybe even a drug issue. I know what it's like. I've been there. Drugs and alcohol use are not only systemic with rock'n'roll bands, they're also rampant in country bands. It's a downward spiral that will wreck your life."

He lifted her chin. "Your life is worth so much more. Don't let alcohol wreck it. Can you admit you have a drinking addiction? Will you make the changes necessary to improve your life?"

The look of compassion and care in Michael's eyes melted her heart. It brought back memories of all the times he had encouraged her when she was going through the audition process for "America's Next Best Talent." Then her memories shifted to recalling how Neil became belligerent when drinking and she knew in her heart she had done the same. "I don't know what's happened to me, Michael."

Her voice choked with emotion. "I had such high hopes for being in the band. but it didn't turn out the way I expected. I don't wanna end up like Neil and lose my friends, and most importantly you. Please forgive me. Not just for last night but also for the way I tore us apart. I am so sorry. I was so insensitive and stupid."

Michael cupped both hands around her chin. "If I was still on that downward spiral like in my band days, I would have told you to go to blazes. But I've changed. God changed me. As he forgave me for all my wrongs, I can forgive you as well. But you've got to make some changes, so you don't continue to spiral out of control."

Nikki leaned against his shoulder and closed her eyes as tears cascaded down her cheeks. "Oh Michael, I've made such a mess of my life. I know I need to change. What can I do to make it better?"

"You just had a breakthrough moment, or a moment of clarity as they say in AA. Are you willing to do what it takes to get out from under your addiction? And understand that it is an addiction."

Nikki looked at him with a feeling mixed of anxiety and hope. "The drugs and alcohol aren't improving my life, only making matters worse. What can I do? Can you help me make a change?"

Michael shook his head. "I can't do this *for you*. You need to want to change. I'll help you walk through it, but it's got to be a commitment on your part. No pretending to change. Are you willing to do that?"

"Yes." Nikki nodded her head several times. "I don't like the way my life's been heading. I was somewhat relieved when Neil went into rehab because I knew that would give me time to work on my life as well. What's the next step I need to take?"

"Funny that you should say it that way. There's a step study meeting for AA tonight at the church. I think you should go. The people you'll meet are those who've gone through downward spirals like you and some even worse. You don't have to say anything. You can just sit there and listen. That's how the healing and change begins.

"Can you go with me for moral support?" Nikki asked imploringly.

"Of course, I can, and I'll stop you from running out the door screaming."

Nikki's eyes grew big, her lips quivered. "Why? Why would I run out the door screaming?"

"Absolutely no reason at all." Michael grinned. "But this isn't a one meeting cure all. You'll need to keep going to the meetings, follow the step study, and be willing to honestly make amends to those you've hurt with more than a casual I'm sorry and let's forget it. Can you do that?"

Nikki twirled a bit of her hair around her finger and scrunched up her face. What Michael was asking of her sounded like a tall order. A real change of heart. How many times had she responded with a half-hearted "I'm sorry" and blame it on the alcohol. Alcohol was really messing up her life. Could she really change? Michael got control of his life. Maybe she could, too.

Standing there, Nikki felt a bubbling of hope and a bit of anxiety. Michael hadn't given up on her. He suggested a way to make her life better, which she desperately needed. Would it be possible for them to be together again not just for AA meetings?

Chapter 8

Later that evening, Nikki was a bundle of nerves as she thought about the AA meeting. Was she really an alcoholic? Sure, she could toss down several drinks in an evening. Wasn't that just de-stressing? Why should she stop drinking altogether? Wasn't that a bit harsh? So far, she hadn't had any alcohol since she spoke to Michael. Didn't that prove that she wasn't an alcoholic?

Yet Michael's words echoed in her head. He had said that alcoholics may not drink for a few days, but once they start, one drink is never enough, and they don't know when to stop. So maybe she was an alcoholic. Using alcohol as a coping mechanism didn't solve anything, just masked it for a while. He had been so honest about how alcohol and drugs damaged his life by getting into verbal and physical fights with band members and people at bars, to drunk driving arrests, and waking up in places he had no idea how we got there or what happened the night before.

Though she never got into fights herself, she could relate to the not remembering what happened the night before and reaching for a drink anytime she got upset. How would she change that? Michael said to take it one step at a time and that started with being open and honest about her addiction.

The sound of her cell phone ringing made Nikki jump. Seeing it was Michael's number, she relaxed. "Still picking me up for the meeting?"

"Yes. Wanted to make sure you didn't have cold feet. See you soon."

"Great. I'm a bit nervous. Glad you'll be with me."

"Don't overthink this. Keep remembering it's one step at a time."

Nikki heard Michael's entrance to the apartment ten minutes later as her mom opened the door and greeted him. "Hello, Mrs. McLellan, good to see you." "Just call me Dania like my guests do.
We've known each other long enough."

"If that's what you prefer, Dania."

"I'm ready to go," Nikki said as she joined them and put on her coat.

"So, what are you two up to tonight?"

Nikki turned and stared at Michael, waiting for his response.

"We're headed over to the church. I want to show Nikki some of the music I've been working on for the Christmas program and get her thoughts."

Nikki quickly nodded agreement.

"That sounds lovely. Maybe you could convince her to even be a part of it."

"Let's not rush things, Mom. See you later." After she gave her mom a quick peck on the cheek, she and Michael headed out the door. Once inside the car, Nikki squeezed Michael's arm. "Thank you for coming up with something to say to my mom. I was at a loss. I'm not ready to tell her about the meeting. I want to see if it makes sense to me.""

What I said to your mom wasn't a lie. I do want to show you the music after the meeting and get your reactions."

The meeting was not in the church sanctuary as Nikki had expected. It took place in the education building where they had Thursday night Bible studies for adults. When they walked in, there were 25 to 30 people milling about the room. At the back of the room, there was a setup for coffee and cookies.

People smiled and welcomed her as they passed by. But no one stared at her or whispered, "What's she doing here?' She breathed a sigh of relief seeing there wasn't an attendance sign-in sheet. There would be no written record that she was there, but then the meeting was for Alcoholics Anonymous, not about who you were.

As they took their seats, a man in his thirties stood in front of a podium and everyone quieted down.

"Let's all bow our heads for a moment of silence. Then Trevor will lead us in the serenity prayer."

Saying the serenity prayer came as a surprise to Nikki since the prayer started off with God. She thought AA was some sort of eastern mysticism thing. Instead, God was front and center with that prayer.

After the prayer was complete, the man at the podium spoke again." Hello, my name is Mason and I'm an alcoholic. Are there other alcoholics in this room?"

Nikki was surprised to see that everyone in the room raised their hand and timidly she raised her hand as well. When she did, Michael gently squeezed her other hand and smiled at her. That calmed her nerves, but her face still turned a light shade of red knowing her palms were sweaty.

"Don't worry," Michael whispered. "You'll get through this."

Mason continued. "Tonight's study is step number two. Wesley would you please read it?"

Nikki's glanced back and forth across the room. Everyone was opening their books to a bookmarked section. She didn't have a book. She thought the book Michael brought with him was a Bible, but he pointed to the page and gestured for her to read with him.

Wesley cleared his throat then said, "Step two, came to believe that a Power greater than ourselves could restore us to sanity" He shook his head and let out a deep breath. "Man, that's a hard one. It's so easy to be full of pride and think we can take care of our own problems and not need anyone else. That's insanity right there.

When I was drinking, the bottle had power over me, not me over it. I had to have it knocked into my thick skull that I was powerless over alcohol and had to let go and let God. That wasn't easy to do. The alcohol was messing up my life. Coming to that realization finally started changing the way I saw life."

Nikki listened as the others gave their thoughts on the step. Hearing how openly they shared about their alcohol issues and in some cases, mentioned drug issues, stunned her. Their stories were telling her story. *How would I manage my life if I stopped drinking? Hope they don't call on me. I'm not ready to share my personal life with these strangers. But their honesty and hope for a better life shows a real commitment to the program. Maybe it could make a change in my life as well.*

As the meeting ended, Nikki relaxed and let go of the anxiety she had built up, fearing that someone would call on her to speak. Before people left, she heard the group say in unison, "Keep coming back. It works if you work it, and it won't if you don't." That got Nikki thinking. *Am I willing to make a commitment to stop drinking or is this simply a wish with no action behind it?*

"Ready to go, Nicole?"

Nikki turned to face Michael. "Sure. Sorry I was just deep in thought."

"That often happens in these meetings. Would you like to go over to the choir room, play some music, and talk?"

"Sure. This meeting wasn't anything like I expected. I mean I knew the part about people saying they were alcoholics because I've seen that on TV and in the movies, but the stories they shared about how much of a wreck alcohol made of their lives got to me."

"It was that way for me, too. At first, I tried to rationalize that I wasn't as bad as some of them. That I could stop drinking anytime. But that's the devil whispering a lie in your ear. Once alcoholics pick up their first drink, they can't stop until they're drunk. Although they won't accept that they're drunk. It's just those obnoxious people around them who exaggerate how much they're drinking." Michael gave her a wink and chuckled.

When they reached the door to the auditorium, he pulled it open, but stopped for a moment. "Can you think of a time in the last few years that you stopped drinking after one drink? And you can't count stopping after one drink as you head out the door to meet someone if you continue drinking once you get there."

Nikki's mouth fell open and then she became tight lipped. How could he ask such a thing? Her mind raced over several past instances of drinking trying to prove to herself and to him that she could control her drinking.

"No need to give me an answer right now, Nicole. Just think about it for a few minutes as we walk to the stage."

They continued to walk silently until they came to the piano and Michael sat down on the bench with Nikki sitting in a chair nearby. She crossed her arms over her chest and leaned back. "Are you judging me? Do you think you're better than me?"

Michael replied tenderly, "Not at all. My first sponsor asked me that same question. Like you, I showed my annoyance when asked if I could control my drinking. I racked my brain for examples of how I had stopped, but I found none. My guess that's the same result you had."

Nikki nodded and unfolded her arms putting them in her lap. "Why can't it be like when we were teenagers?"

Michael began playing a song they sang in one of their high school musicals. "Wouldn't it be grand? If I could just take your hand, as we walked along the strand –

Nikki sang along with Michael "Watching the waves hit the sand. Oh. how lovely that would be, if once again we could be… in dreamland."

Michael stopped singing but continued to play the piano. "So, you remember the lyrics, too."

Nikki laughed. "How could I not? We must have rehearsed them one thousand times. I think the songs from Dreamland are permanently embedded in my brain."

They sang several more songs from their past musicals as they laughed and reminisced. And as they did, Michael cast sideways glances at Nicole remembering how much they were in love at one time and the plans they had for the future.

There was one plan he never had the chance to tell her. He was going to ask her to marry him the weekend she got her big break, but she left town before he had the chance to show her the ring and propose. He still had that ring in the top drawer of his dresser.

Chapter 9

The next morning Nikki woke with a smile on her face. One reason was she didn't have a hangover from last night. The second reason was she enjoyed her time with Michael. Singing together brought back all the good times they had in high school.

Getting out of bed, she pulled a box from her closet. She removed one of the scrapbooks inside. It held the program for *Dreamland,* a playbill, the music score, a publicity shot of the full cast, and a photo album of impromptu pictures of cast members with notes written underneath each of them.

She stopped turning the pages when she found the one of Michael. Below his picture he had written, "Being with you is like being in Dreamland. And it's a dream I never want to leave. Hope our future is a beautiful dreamland." She ran her fingers slowly over those words and read them again as a tear fell from her eye. *Oh, what a mess I made of things. That's all in my past and I can't change it. In a few weeks I'll be back with the band and Michael will remain here as the church music director. That's just how life happens.*

Her phone rang. Seeing it was from Michael, she wiped away the tear and quickly answered it. "Hey music man, what's up?"

"Sounds like you had a good sleep. Were you singing all night in your dreams?"

"Don't remember my dreams, but I do remember the fun we had playing songs together last night."

"Yeah, so many great memories. After attending your first AA meeting, are you ready to try another one today?"

"Another one? Isn't it like going to church where you only do it once a week?"

Michael laughed. "Well, some of us do come to church more than once a week with either Bible studies or midweek services. However, as a newbie AA participant, it's suggested you attend daily meetings for the first 90 days to help reinforce your commitment. Especially with the holidays and so many opportunities to slip and drink."

Nikki hadn't considered that, but it made sense. Soon she'd be back on tour with the band. She would need to create a new habit of not drinking. "Do they have AA meetings outside of the country? Did you get sober while you were still in 'Gone South'?"

"Meetings are held day and night in most major cities. They've got an app that lists where meetings occur. I'll text you the link so you can have it handy. My sobriety started between tours when I was writing music and it was a godsend. And that's when I found Jesus, too. "Wow, a double whammy. You really jumped in with two feet."

That's really not unusual. Step two last night talked about finding a higher power greater than ourselves. The ultimate higher power is Jesus. Finding faith again wasn't a giant leap. It was more of a welcome home. It gave me the joy and hope I couldn't find in fame."

Listening to Michael she could tell he really meant it. He wasn't just spouting the right words. But faith? The only faith she had was in believing in herself. But her decisions weren't always the best ones. She hadn't become a superstar as she had hoped by this time in her life, but she was in a top band that could fill stadiums. "Yes, fame is a tricky thing. But it seems like you found your perfect niche."

"You will too Nicole. Open your heart to the plans God has for you. So, are you up for another meeting? Grace Methodist on Oak Glen has one at 3:00 o'clock today. It's a discussion meeting, but you won't have to speak, just listen. Afterwards, we could go have a quick bite then you could come with me to my rehearsal with the kids in the Christmas program. They'd get a real kick in seeing a hometown celebrity."

She didn't know if she was ready for another meeting but since Michael thought it was a good idea, why not go? "Maybe I should meet you at the other church. That way I'll just stay a little bit for your rehearsals, so I don't get in the way."

"Sure. Let's meet at Grace Methodist at 2:45. If you're not there 15 minutes early, you're considered late."

After ending the call, Nikki carefully returned all the items to her special box. Those high school years held precious memories. Then she focused only on her music future and forgot what really was important. *That's gotta change. I'm going to focus on the now and make me a better person.*

Chapter 10

When Nikki sauntered into the inn's dining room an hour later, her mom was busy cleaning up after the breakfast with her guests. "Did you have a good time with Michael last night?"

Nikki picked up one of the two croissants left on a tray and added some jam and clotted cream to it. "Mom, these are as heavenly as ever. You should sell these to Kayla's coffee house. They'd be a hit."

"And where would I find the time to do that extra baking on top of running this inn? Now if you were here to help – "

"Mom, you know I have another job that keeps me on the road. I make a fairly good living at it. If you need the money to hire an assistant, I'd be happy to help."

"Heavens no! I'm fine with the staff I have. I just don't need to add more work to what's needed. "Now tell me about last night" She picked up a coffee cup and motioned for Nikki to join her at a nearby table.

"It was fun. Michael played a bunch of songs from our high school musicals, and we sang along together. Surprising how easy it was to remember the lyrics. We still had good harmonies, too."

"I'm sure Michael could add a number to the Christmas program as a duet for the two of you."

Nikki waved her hand dismissively. "Those days are long gone. We're not part of the same world anymore."

Mom patted Nikki's hand. "But you were such a great couple. I'd love to hear the two of you singing together again, even for only one song. And I know many others in town would enjoy it as well."

"How could I ask that of Michael? It would sound like I'm trying to be a diva and tell the whole town, "Hey look at me the big star." He doesn't need to do me any special favors."

"Well, I think it would be a wonderful idea. Just ask him. Don't make a big deal out of it." Mom got up with her tray and walked toward the kitchen. "There's some leftover fruit cup from this morning if you want some. What are your plans for today?"

"I noticed there were still a few boxes of Christmas stuff in the office not yet put out. Want me to do that this morning?"

"Yes, thanks. Let me put these last few items where they belong and I'll join you."

The boxes held hand painted miniature ceramic village stores and the snow-like carpet of tufted cotton balls. Together they created a centerpiece for the dining room. They added a smaller assortment at the back of the credenza.

Next, they hung garlands over the door frames and brought out two 5-foot tall wooden toy soldiers to flank the credenza.

Looking at what they created, Nikki smiled. The room had a wonderful festive feel to it with their added décor to go along with the small tables that were adorned with dark green tablecloths and topped with cranberry and greenery candle rings. "I haven't done this much Christmas decorating in the last seven years. Going from one event to another, we were too tired to decorate. We had an itty-bitty artificial tree on the table in the bus and a few silver garlands strewn here and there. Not very festive at all."

"We'll be having the town's tree lighting later this week. After that, we'll decorate a big tree in the inn's great room with any guests who want to help. Delivery will be the day of the tree lighting. Would love you to join in, too."

Nikki hugged her mom. "I remember the fun we had doing that with the guests over the years. That will be great memories when I'm back on the road. Now, I have plans to meet Kayla, maybe do a little Christmas shopping, and get together with some of my old friends this evening. Don't count on me for dinner."

"Enjoy yourself!"

Nikki headed back to her room to get her coat. She didn't like lying to her mom, but she wasn't ready to tell her about going to the AA meetings. But she planned to talk to Kayla about it.

When Nikki arrived at Coffee Haven & Sweets, she was happy to see there was a temporary lull in customers as the only one remaining was in the process of leaving the store. Nikki walked straight to the counter and pointed to one of the few remaining green and red sprinkled coffee crumble squares. "Glad there's one more for me. Plus my regular chai. How's your day been?"

"Busy. Glad to have a break. As long as no one else comes in, I'll sit with you. It'll be good to get off my feet."

Looking down at her plate and cutting a small piece of the crumble square with her fork, Nikki said, "Umm, you know Neil from the band is in drug rehab. And I was thinking that I might need some help with alcohol addiction. Do you know anything about Alcoholics Anonymous?"

"Yeah, I'm familiar with the program." Kayla took a bite of a cherry Danish.

"Sooo, what do you know about it?"

"I know it only works if the person has a true commitment to following the program and not drinking. It'll work if you work at it, but it won't if you don't."

Nikki's head jerked up when she heard Kayla's words. It was so similar to what she heard at the meeting last night. "Isn't that kind of harsh telling people they can't drink at all."

"Let me show you something." Kayla picked up her phone and scrolled through it. "If you want to know if you're an alcoholic, or you think somebody else you know might be an alcoholic, honestly answer these 12 questions."

Nikki drew closer to read the list on Kayla's phone as she sipped her chai. The questions talked about getting drunk when you didn't mean to, having blackouts, promising to quit, then going back to drinking, and other similar questions. In Nikki's mind, she answered ten out of the twelve as yes.

"If the person gets three or more as a yes, they have a problem with drinking. How many of these did you answer yes to, Nikki?"

Nikki leaned back and wrapped both hands around the hot mug. "Why would you think I answered yes to any of these questions? I was asking this for Neil."

"C'mon Nikki I was there the other night when you got drunk. Drinking is a problem for you."

"That's hard for me to admit. I think I can control my drinking, but apparently, I can't. How do you know about these AA questions?"

"You know Michael had a drinking problem when he was touring, right? After he got sober, he asked about opening the church doors to AA groups. Luke and I went to some meetings with him to check it out."

"He took me to an AA meeting last night. We're going to another one later this afternoon." Kayla raised an eyebrow and smiled. "Really? The program works for Michael. Hope it does for you. Other than AA, how are things going with you two?"

Nikki felt the heat rise on her face. "Going to an AA meeting is hardly a date, but we did end up playing songs from our old high school musicals, which was a lot of fun."

"Did that rekindle the romance that once was?"

"It brought up old memories. But that's the past. Soon I'll be back on tour, and he'll be here." Nikki shook her head. "There's no future in that."

Kayla leaned in and stared at Nikki intently. "Do you want a future with him? A second chance to rewrite your life together?"

Nikki leaned back in her chair and shrugged. "Last night did bring back the memories of what we once had. But we've both changed and moved on."

"You're not married or have a boyfriend, do you?"

"No, but --,

"Michael isn't married and he's not in a relationship either. You're both open to starting again. That is if you both want it. I think Michael wants another chance, and you probably do as well. What are you going to do about it?"

"Nothing. I'm going to enjoy the Christmas season. Spend time with my friends and my mom. Just live in the present and not try to redo the past."

Nikki's phone buzzed. "Oops. Gotta run. That's my reminder to meet Michael and I added in a little time for shopping." Nikki stood and hugged Kayla.

"I'll send up a few prayers for you, Nikki, that you'll find a way to incorporate your present into a better future. Have a good time with Michael."

As Kayla picked up the empty plates and mugs, Nikki walked out the door shaking her head. Even if she wanted to have a new relationship with Michael, she knew long distance relationships never worked. They usually ended with bitterness between the two parties. She had done that once to Michael and she didn't want to do it again.

Chapter 11

Once outside on the sidewalk, Nikki wove her way through the crowds of shoppers laden with Christmas bags who made abrupt stops when something caught their eye in a window display. Soon she found herself doing the same thing as she lingered from storefront to storefront.

Then she noticed a new store, The Bakers Choice - Tools for Home and Pro Chefs. She did a quick scan of the front window and decided this would be a good place to find something for her mom.

"Nicole... Nicole McClellan? Is that you?" That voice seemed awfully familiar. When Nikki turned around to face the woman who spoke, she saw it was her high school music director. She gave the woman a hug. "Mrs. Anderson it's great to see you."

"And it's wonderful to see you again. You were always one of my favorite students. Are you back in town for a visit? Or have you moved back?"

"I'm here through Christmas."

"Our town really knows how to celebrate Christmas. I can't imagine being anywhere else for the holiday. Did you know that Michael Wilkerson has returned as well, but not just for a visit."

Mrs. Anderson barely gave Nikki a chance to do anything else but nod before she continued her one-sided conversation. "I'm proud to say that he's the music director at Abundant Life Church.

You two were the perfect duo. Your harmonies made my job so much easier. And the chemistry between the two of you on stage was spectacular. But of course, we both know it was more than just acting. It was evident that you had a romantic connection both on and off the stage.

You know, seeing how you two were in high school, I expected to see your wedding announcement within the next couple of years, but that didn't happen. I guess it just goes to show that young love doesn't always end up as lasting love."

Nikki's eyes welled with tears, and she remembered how they had talked about getting married until fame got in the way. With a lump in her throat, she silently nodded.

Mrs. Anderson threw her hands over her mouth. "Oh, dear me. I've upset you. I just can't help myself. I tend to prattle on too much when I run into my old students. Please forgive me."

"Nothing to forgive." Nikki willed away the tears and attempted a slight smile. "You're right. What we had was teenage crush without the depth of lasting romantic love. Now we both love the careers we've chosen for ourselves so that makes up for it."

"Well, that's good to hear." Mrs. Anderson gave a slight squeeze to Nikki's arm. "You have careers that you love just as much as I enjoy teaching. It's been good seeing you again. I'm so proud of you. Have a wonderful Christmas."

They parted ways and Nikki decided to come back to Bakers Choice another time. Right now, her heart wasn't into buying gifts. What she really wanted was to have a drink and dull the ache she felt, but that wouldn't do. She had made a commitment to go to an AA meeting with Michael and wouldn't renege on that promise.

She checked the time on her Fitbit and kept moving. *I need to focus on something else. What were the words of that step from last night? Something about God and insanity. No, that wasn't right to equate God to insanity.*

It was something about believing and being restored. That's what I need.

Then the words flashed across her mind as if written on a screen...Came to believe that a Power greater than ourselves could restore us to sanity. *I don't know anything I want to call the higher power like Buddha or Krishna, they don't seem to fit. Michael talks about God. That sounds like a start for a higher power. Hmmm. For me, it would be... I came to believe that God could restore me to sanity.* She repeated that line over and over until she arrived at the corner where Grace Methodist Church was located.

She stopped and took a deep breath. Looking up at the church, she closed her eyes and silently said what was probably her first prayer. "God, if you are really there, I sure could use your mighty help. Can you really restore me to sanity where life makes sense and has meaning which doesn't require alcohol to keep me numb? I truly need that. Amen."

When she opened her eyes, she noticed Michael standing outside the double doors on the top of the steps waving at her. This time she felt happy about going to an AA meeting. She ran up the steps to meet him. Butterflies were twirling about in her stomach over what this meeting would be like, but her heart beat a steady rhythm knowing Michael would be there with her.

Chapter 12

Nikki was smiling as the meeting ended and Michael helped her with her coat. "Michael, this is not what I expected AA meetings to be like. I thought they'd be somber and preachy, and they would feel like they would never end. Instead, people are laughing and engaging with each other. It's like they're all family."

"Well, in a lot of ways, it is like family. We're here to support and encourage one another. And like family, we have our stories to tell of the stupid stuff we've done before we got sober as cautionary tales for others."

"You mean like the guy who was tossed out of the mission outreach for being disorderly and drunk and now is the mission's director. Or the woman who in sobriety discovered she had a master's degree and did her verbal in a blackout and is now a social worker helping other alcoholics get sober."

"Two great examples of lives changed for the better rather than continuing to do the irrational stuff we considered rational when drinking."

The meeting's leader walked over to Nikki. "Here's your copy of the big book. The other alcoholics at this meeting have written their names and numbers in it. Call any of them if you feel like you're going to slip and have a drink. They're available whenever you need them."

Nikki gave him a quick hug. "Thanks. Much appreciated."

Michael shook his hand, then put his arm around Nikki's back and headed out of the meeting. "I didn't see you drive in. Where are you parked?"

"I spent some time with Kayla and built in shopping time. But my plans changed. Instead, I decided I needed a good walk. Are you in the parking lot?"

"Yes, Let's take my car. We'll get yours after rehearsal tonight."

Nikki slapped her hand to her head. "I forgot about the rehearsal. That's why I should have driven."

"You're not backing out. I know the kids would be ecstatic about meeting a celebrity. I won't keep you out late."

Nikki shook a finger at him. "You'd better take me to some place nice for dinner. It can't be Sal's. From the way I supposedly acted, I don't think they'd be happy to see me." Her smile sagged and she clutched Michael's arm. "I know I acted horribly toward you. I'm terribly sorry. I don't ever want that to happen again."

Michael rubbed his hand gently along the side of her face. "I know. It was hurtful, but I forgive you. When you work the program steps, you learn about making amends and forgiveness." He tapped her on the nose and winked. "Now let's get something to eat. How about the Buttercup Café? They have burgers, soups, salads, and all sorts of great comfort food."

Nikki squeezed his arm. "Wow. They're still in business? We celebrated our high school graduation there. We spent hours talking about our future."

"The server had to tell us they were closing. We didn't even notice all the other tables were empty."

Nikki laughed. "It was like we were in our own Dreamland."

They nodded to each other and began softly singing and recreating the dance steps they did back in the high school musical. "Wouldn't it be grand? If I could just take your hand, as we walked along the strand. Watching the waves hit the sand. Oh, how lovely that would be, if once again we could be… in Dreamland."

Then Michael gave Nikki a twirl and pulled her back into his arms like they had done back then. Nikki's heart pounded as they moved closer, and their lips met. The touch was gentle at first, like a first kiss, but then the kiss deepened. Nikki's whole body began to tingle.

As they finally separated, Nikki's eyes fluttered open to find Michael gazing at her intently. "Um, that wasn't like how we did it in the musical," he said.

Nikki leaned her head into Michael's chest and breathlessly added, "No, it was more like the times we kissed as we discussed our future. Just as wonderful."

Michael lifted her chin. "You still remember those kisses?"

"Of course, I do. Don't you?"

"I've never forgotten them, or you."
Michael gazed deeply into her eyes. "You
know, I've never stopped loving you."

Nikki rested her hands on his chest and
sighed. "You were my first love. We never get
over our first love, but we've both grown up
and changed."

"Do you still have feelings for me?"

"Yes - -

"Good. That's something that hasn't
changed. We can build on that again."

Nikki pushed herself away from him and
held her arms out to her side. "C'mon Michael,
let's not kid ourselves. What we had as teens
was special, but our lives have changed. Your
life is here as a church music director and
mine is playing in a band that tours
everywhere." "We'll have a long-distance
romance." Michael held her hands in his. "We'll
call and talk constantly."

"Long distance romances only work in the short run and then they fizzle out. I don't want us to hurt each other like that."

"And I don't want to lose you again."

Holding his hands sent jolts of electricity through her body. Yes, she still loved him, but their lives were only meant to intersect for the few weeks she'd be home. It was all too confusing. *I need a drink to calm down and focus. No. There will be no drinking.* "I don't know Michael, I …"

"Let's take it one day at a time. You're going through a big transition with getting sober. We'll have time to sort the rest out later."

Nikki nodded and shivered. "This is winter. We're not on a stage set. I'm cold."

Michael held her close and kissed her softly. "Does that warm you up?"

"You know it does." Nikki looked longingly into his eyes. *How can a simple kiss make me want to melt like a snowball? Why was I so blind to walk away from what we had? I can't hurt him like that again. Got to keep my distance until I know what's going on with the band.* "How about we get some food and warm up?"

It was just a short drive to the Buttercup Café. The sizzling of grilled hamburgers and French fries enticed their taste buds as they entered. The classic oldies songs sounded like a whisper under the chatter and laughter of people enjoying their meals. Luckily, a large group of people had just left, and the staff was busy reconfiguring the table setups for two and four people. While waiting, they huddled close to review a menu.

"Oh look," Nikki said. "They have chicken pot pie. On a cold wintry night like tonight, that fits the bill for me."

I'd rather have breakfast for dinner, which they serve all day. Their blueberry muffin pancakes are amazing with their chicken apple sausages."

"Can we share like we used to?"

"I'm good with that if you are."

The hostess called their name and they walked to their table. Along the way Michael waved to families he knew.

Once they sat and the server took their order, Nikki asked, "Are the people you greeted and waved to, members of the church?"

"Yes. You get to know a lot of people when you're in charge of the music ministry. I get to know parents, kids, and adults who like to sing. It's like having a large extended family. I'm so blessed to be a part of it."

Nikki reached over and squeezed his hand. "I can see how much it means to you. But don't you miss performing for thousands of fans?"

A big grin stretched across Michael's face. "Maybe when I first walked away from it and was trying to get sober, but certainly not these days. I have such a joy and peace about what I'm doing. It's great knowing I'm doing something that matters."

Nikki considered what he said. *Did playing music with her band matter? Not really. When was the last time I felt I was doing something that mattered?*

"Here's your coffee and tea," said their server. "Your food will be out shortly."

They sipped their drinks, then Nikki asked, "What do you enjoy most about being the music director?"

"That's easy. Working with the teens. At that age they're looking for acceptance and direction. I love seeing their eyes light up when they connect to the idea I'm trying to convey. That's why I want you to meet them tonight. Some definitely have star potential. I want to make sure they don't forget who they are and what's important."

"What do you want me to do?"

"Encourage them and their singing. Give them professional tips. One singer to another. And I'll do my best to prevent them from peppering you with hundreds of questions about what it's like being a music star."

Nikki laughed. "I haven't done any meet and greets with fans in a long time. This should be interesting."

Their server delivered their entrees and Michael said a short blessing over the food before they dug into it.

Praying before meals is new to me, but it seems natural to him. What made him change so much?

"Nicole, have you decided against sharing? I just asked you about trying some of these pancakes and you ignored me."

Nikki's head snapped up. Her thoughts were elsewhere, and she hadn't heard what he said. "Sorry, mental cul-de-sac. This is as good as I remembered."

"So are the pancakes. Take a bite and see what else you've been missing. and I'll take a scoop of your pot pie."

As they ate and shared samples from each other's plates, it was as if they turned back time to when they were teenagers and happily living in the moment. Nikki wished they could sit there for hours, but Michael was keeping track of time so they wouldn't be late for his rehearsal.

Chapter 13

When Nikki and Michael arrived at the church, teens were already chatting and laughing while they waited for the rehearsal to begin. As he walked down toward the front of the room, he bellowed in a theatrical voice, "Good evening my diligent performers. Ready to make a joyful noise and give praise to the Lord?"

Cheers and applause erupted as the students began to take their places.

Nikki whispered to Michael, "It's amazing how these kids are so excited about you directing them."

Michael whispered back, "They're a lot like we were, except here we sing songs to glorify God and praise him for what he's done in our lives."

Preachy music? What had she gotten herself into? She thought they would be singing songs like "I'm Dreaming of a White Christmas,"
"Santa Claus is Coming to Town," and "Jingle Bells."

"Okay ladies and gentlemen as you can see, we have a guest tonight." Michael did a theatrical wave toward her. "And I want you to be on your best behavior to make me look good."

Snickers, giggles, and smiles wove through the singers as Michael stepped to the piano and sat.

One student timidly raised her hand and getting a nod from Michael asked, "Are you gonna tell us who your guest is? Is she your girlfriend?"

Nikki's eyes grew wide, and her mouth dropped open. *These kids were certainly direct in their questions.*

Michael began to play background music on the keys as he started his answer. "Girlfriend, yes, back in the day when we were your age. Then we took different paths in music. She's currently on break between tours with a band called 'Lockwood & Sutton.' You have a bona fide star in your midst."

Lots of wows and applause broke out as excitement surged through the group. Nikki smiled and waved to them. "I'm excited to hear what you've got. When Michael and I were back in high school, we did musicals together and auditioned for anything that gave us the opportunity to sing. So let me see your star quality shine."

She watched as the students stood tall and grinned with confidence hoping they had that star quality and could make a career in music.

That's what it was like for her in high school. She had hoped for that magical moment of being discovered. "America's Best New Talent" gave her that opportunity and it changed her life dramatically.

As she glanced over at Michael, she wondered what her life would have been like if she hadn't done that audition and had gone on the road with him instead. She liked country songs and could easily imagine the two of them singing duets in the band, but that was a missed opportunity.

"Let's begin with 'Mary Did You Know' with the boys starting off the first question and then the girls will come in at the next question and continue alternating male to female until we end together. This time each group try to remember to sing only your part, not the other side as well, okay?"

Nikki was not familiar with the song, but she found herself listening intently to each of the questions and started to wonder what it was like to be Jesus' mom. The song made Mary seem real to her. She continued to listen intently as he led the singers through several other songs which weren't familiar either.

They included songs called "It's Christmas," "The Heart of Christmas," and "Christmas This Year." Then he played "Joy to the World, Unspeakable Joy" which had parts to it she had heard. This rehearsal was not what she had expected. She was impressed by the way he had arranged the music to bring out the harmonies and solos. He had a bona fide talent for being a musical director.

When they were ready to take a break, one of the girls raised her hand. "Mr. Wilkerson did the two of you ever sing any Christmas songs together?"

Nikki's heart skipped a beat as she looked over and smiled at Michael. Singing Christmas tunes with him was always the highlight of her Christmas season growing up.

"We sang at the Christmas tree lighting, did caroling together, and of course our school's Christmas program."

Multiple questions began to erupt from the group. "Could you sing one for us?"

"Yes, would you?"

"That would be fun to hear."

"Please sing a song?"

Michael threw up his hands. "Sounds like we still have an audience for our duets. Want to give it a go for them?"

Nikki shrugged. "What have we got to lose?" Then she turned and raised an eyebrow as she pointed her finger. "Now there will not be any videos with your cell phones. This is for your ears only. We haven't rehearsed in years."

The whole group nodded repeatedly and murmurs of "no videos" passed through the young singers.

Michael randomly played notes on the piano and waved Nikki over. "Let's do a perennial favorite, 'Winter Wonderland.' We certainly sang that together many times. Come have a seat by me."

Michael started the intro to "Winter Wonderland" as Nikki walked over and sat. They discussed the harmonies for a minute and then began singing, "Sleigh bells ring…" They didn't make a big production out of it like she would have if she were singing in concert with her band. Instead, this performance was done for the pure joy of harmonizing with her best friend and once boyfriend.

When the song ended, all the teens broke out in applause.

Nikki felt a bit giddy like when she was a teenager and saw her parents and friends applauding her in the school auditorium. She leaned over and bumped shoulders with Michael. "That was fun. Just like the old days."

Michael gave her a wink. "You know it could be that way again."

There was hope and promise wrapped in those words. For a moment, Nikki wished they were back in school again when the promise of their future together was real.

Becoming aware of the silence in the room and all his students staring at them, Michael cleared his throat and raised his voice for the kids to hear, as he turned toward Nikki. "Since you'll be in town through the holiday, why don't you help me with the Christmas program? It would be fun to do it together. What do you say?"

Nikki wanted to send the kids home even without the rehearsal being complete so they could talk without interruption. But that wasn't possible. This wasn't about her. It was about the kids being at their best for their Christmas performance. Her talents and abilities would be a benefit to them. She turned to the kids and spread out her arms. "Would you like me to work as an assistant director?"

Her answer came as applause and grins from all the singers.

"Looks like you'll be stuck with me for a while," Nikki said to Michael.

"Suits me just fine. Let's get back to rehearsing."

For the next hour, Nikki listened carefully as each teen took turns singing their part and offered gentle guidance on how to improve their pitch and tone. Watching them sing, she noticed the bright and eager expressions on their faces, their eyes sparkling with excitement and joy. She could see their passion and dedication to the music, and she forgot that they were singing praises to God and not of Santa Claus or snowmen.

When Michael ended the rehearsal, she was surprised at how quickly the time had passed. As the teens left, they waved and thanked her for the time she spent with them. This touched her heart more than having thousands of screaming fans cheering for the band.

Once they were alone, she plopped in a chair closest to the piano. "That was utterly amazing. I loved watching the kids' faces as they caught on to how we were leading them with the music. I even liked the songs they sang and forgot it was church music."

"Do you have something against church music?" Michael asked with a wry grin.

Nikki felt the heat rising on her face. "No, um, I, oh, I thought church music had all those thys and thous and a droning beat with no real rhythm, just heavy organ chords."

Michael leaned back and laughed. "You haven't spent much time in church, have you? I mostly play the piano, but at some events I play the organ. The songs you refer to as having a lot of the thys and thous are called hymns.

Many of those hymns have a strong biblical context and have been given a more modern beat to touch the hearts of those who haven't been to church and inspire those who regularly attend. The songs we sing today are known as praise songs. When we play them, I'll lead with my guitar and we'll have a bass player, a drummer, and maybe a sax or a horn with singers."

"Well," Nikki rolled her eyes. "Whatever you call them, I liked them even if I only heard the version with a piano."

"Thanks. Here's one of my favorites. The message is one you'd hear in a traditional hymn, but its lyrical style is contemporary." Michael turned back to the piano and played several introductory bars before beginning the lyrics of "How Great Is Our God."

Nikki sat in rapt attention as Michael played his heart and soul into that song. It was evident that he believed the words he was singing. She could feel its message sinking deep into her heart. *This God, Michael sings about, was someone I could believe in. But why would he accept me? My only church attendance has been Easter and Christmas events. What would I need to do to obtain his acceptance?* Tears were welling in her eyes as Michael finished the song. She quickly dabbed them away with her fingers, hoping Michael wouldn't notice.

But he did. He reached over and took her hands in his. "What's going on Nicole? What brought on the tears?"

She blinked back tears feeling overwhelmed with a sense of inadequacy. Through teary eyes she whispered, "You really believe what you were singing, don't you Michael? Your God is real to you. How did that happen? Did you do something miraculous that he accepted you?"

Michael held her hands tightly and gazed deeply into her eyes. "Nicole, the only miraculous thing I did was to admit I had made a wreck of my life and was a sinner who needed a savior. I reached out to Jesus, and he answered my prayer. He's as real to me as you are. Is that what you want, Nicole?"

"You know me, Michael. You remember the hopes and dreams I had for my future in singing. Yes, I'm in a top-rated band but it feels like I'm on a treadmill repeating the same things over and over and just not getting anywhere. Drugs, alcohol, or sex hasn't filled the hole I feel inside me. I can see a sense of fulfillment in you that's not just from being a music director. It looks like it's your connection to God. I want that for myself."

Michael smiled and nodded. "I'm happy to hear you say that." Then he pointed to the cross at the front of the room. "The God I serve is Jesus Christ. He suffered and died for my sins, your sins, and everyone else's in the world. He offers forgiveness and acceptance to all who believe in him and repent of their sins. Are you ready to do that?"

Nikki nodded.

"If this is something you truly want, then repeat this prayer after me."

In response, Nikki clenched Michael's hands tightly and bowed her head.

"Lord Jesus, I admit I am a sinner. I am sorry for my sins and the life I have lived; I need your forgiveness. I confess you as my Lord and want to turn away from my sins. Thank you,
Jesus, for saving me and forgiving me! Amen!"

Nicki repeated the words slowly and deliberately after Michael said each sentence. When she finished, she felt a weight lift off her shoulders. There wasn't a choir of angels singing or a bright light shining down upon her, but she felt different. A warmth and tingle of joy filled her heart. She opened her eyes and smiled at Michael. "So, what do I do now? What's the next step?"

"Let me give you a Bible so you can start reading and understanding who Jesus is." He walked over to a box on the side of the stage and picked up a book. "The bookmark in here is at the beginning of the Gospel of John. Even though it's in the middle of book, it's a great place to start."

As he brought it over to her, he added "What you just prayed is something called the sinner's prayer. It's also AA's third step, which is 'Made a decision to turn our will and our lives over to the care of God as we understood Him.' Congratulations on both of those."

Nikki beamed. "This feels good. I hope it lasts."

"It will if you stay focused on Jesus and read the Bible. Start with a couple of chapters tonight before you go to bed. Call me if you have any questions about what you're reading. I'll be happy to answer them."

Nikki clasped the Bible close to her chest. "Thanks for what you just did for me. I'll probably have lots of questions but will try not to overwhelm you with them."

"Whatever questions you have from reading the Bible, I'll always be happy to answer. I want you to have as real a relationship with Jesus as I have."

As they walked out of the room and down the hallway arm in arm, she felt a peace she hadn't experienced before and wanted it to last.

Chapter 14

After Michael drove Nikki back to her car and she returned home, she turned off the car's engine and just sat there for a moment looking at the inn. The architectural style at the front of the inn was done like an Alpine chalet. Lights twinkled up and down the peak with garlands and additional lights draped over the faux balcony.

She'd probably looked at them thousands of times over the years, but tonight she looked at it in a deeper way as wisps of fog and a smattering of snowflakes floated across her view. It felt as if she were safely cocooned in the snow globe. A deep sense of peace and comfort filled her that she could only consider was possible because of the prayer she had said with Michael. "Thank you, Jesus," she whispered. "Show me the way to let this wonderful feeling keep filling my heart."

As she made her way upstairs to their apartment and down the hall, no lights were visible under the door to her mother's bedroom, so she decided to wait until morning to tell her mom about how she had prayed and felt afterwards. She'd wait until all the guests had breakfast and cleaned up so they could rejoice together.

However, it took much will power not to dance and sing her way down the hall for the fireworks of joy that were erupting inside of her. Instead walked quietly back to her bedroom..

Once in her room, Nikki searched her phone for ways she could listen to more of the Christian songs like Michael had played and was surprised to find apps for Christian radio stations and YouTube videos. When she downloaded a station's app, she was happy to hear a song that the teens had sung that evening. Her heart sang with delight feeling the connection to the music. It took a whole lot of willpower not to sing along in her loudest voice. A whisper would suffice for tonight so not to disturb her mom.

After washing up and donning a nightshirt, she made some herbal tea with her electric teapot. Then she stacked pillows on her bed, so she'd be comfortable as she read her Bible. She smirked thinking how absurd this would have been to her just a month ago. Now she wanted to read the Bible as much as she used to love reading fan texts. She couldn't imagine any of her fans being willing to die for her, but the God of the universe did. How humbling and amazing that was.

Nikki held the Bible to her chest and whispered "Okay Jesus, help me understand the words that I read. Let them sink into my heart." She opened to the bookmark and read the quote on it. "May these words of my mouth and the meditation of my heart be pleasing in your sight, Lord, my Rock and my Redeemer- Psalm 19:14."

She read the verse again and decided that would be a good way to start each time she opened the Bible to read.

As Michael directed, she started with chapter one of the book of John. She read it slowly, adding notes on a small pad when she found something she wanted to ask him about. When she came to the third chapter, she repeated verses 16 and 17, "For God so loved the world that he gave his one and only Son, that whoever believes in him shall not perish but have eternal life. For God did not send his Son into the world to condemn the world, but to save the world through him." Then she closed her eyes and whispered, "Thank you Jesus. I'm looking forward to this new way of living my life with you."

She read a couple more chapters but began to yawn and found herself reading verses without being able to concentrate on what they said. She added the bookmark and then reverently closed the Bible and put it on her nightstand. Turning off the light, she slipped into bed and smiled. Before falling to sleep, she said the words she'd memorized from the bookmark.

When she awoke the next morning, she felt more rested after a night's sleep than she had in a long time. Her sleep seemed like resting on a cloud with angels singing her to sleep with a lullaby. She brewed some tea and let it steep while she took a shower. Even though it looked cold and blustery outside, she thought it was a bright and beautiful day.

She slipped on a soft red sweater with miniature snowflakes at the neck and sleeves, pulled on black corduroy pants and her favorite boots. Sorting through her jewelry box she found a pair of poinsettia earrings and a matching pendant. She gave her hair a final brush and approving of her look in the mirror, headed to the inn's kitchen to find her mom.

There were still a couple of guests sitting in the dining room and chatting. Nikki offered them coffee and tea to go, and suggested they do some shopping in town while it was still early, and the crowds would be light. They took her advice and headed toward their rooms for their coats.

She picked up the few remaining plates on the tables and headed into the kitchen. "The dining room is clear of guests. Got a few minutes so we can talk?"

Seeing the big grin on Nikki's face, her mother stopped reviewing her shopping list at the table. "You seem happy today. Did something special happen between you and Michael last night? Are you getting back together?"

Nikki leaned against the kitchen counter and held out her hands as if weighing a balance. "That would be a definite yes and no. Something special did happen, but it wasn't about me and Michael. Though Michael did open my eyes."

She began pacing as she considered what to say next. "With Neil being in rehab I started looking at my own life and realized I was pretty close to going down that same path. Drugs and alcohol were commonplace on the tour. My life was a wreck. And I knew I needed to make a change. The tipping point came that first night when I went to dinner with my friends. My drinking got the worst of me, and I ended up belittling most of them in a nasty way."

"Oh, Nicole, I can't believe you would do that."

Nikki raised her hands in the air. "I'm not proud of what I said. Actually, I don't really remember what I said, but Kayla set me straight the next day. She had to drive me home. Then I ran into Michael, and he confirmed what Kayla had said. He pointed out my actions were those of an alcoholic. He was right though I cringed having to admit it."

"I can't believe you're an alcoholic. I've seen you have a few drinks and get a bit silly, but you're not like one of those people who drink booze out of a paper bag."

Nikki snorted. "You don't have to be homeless to be an alcoholic. Many alcoholics hold down jobs and binge drink on the weekends. But those binges become more frequent. That was my life on tour. Now I've stopped drinking. I've even gone to AA meetings with Michael and some on my own. The people there made me realize I did have a problem, and AA could help me. I'm sober now and it feels good."

"That's wonderful honey. You know, I recall a cousin talking about AA at a family reunion and how good it was for him."

Nikki sat at the table and took her mom's hands in hers. "There's more. I'm working as Michael's assistant for the church's Christmas program."

Her mom's mouth fell open. "You're working on the music program?"

"Don't look so surprised. I'm able to turn over a new leaf. Listening to them rehearse their songs and talking to Michael about his faith in God got to me. And when he sang "How Great Is Our God" while playing the piano, I could see he really believed what he was singing. I wanted that connection with God, too."

Nikki stopped for a moment remembering the emotions she felt at that moment and tears of joy slipped down her face. "Michael helped me say something called a sinner's prayer where I asked Jesus to forgive my sins and accept me." Her voice cracked as she continued, "And he did. Isn't that wonderful."

Her mom wrapped her arms around Nicole as tears fell from her face as well. "My dear sweet Nicole, I've been praying you'd find your way to Jesus. I'm so glad Michael helped open your eyes. That news is the best Christmas present ever. But what about your band?"

"What do you mean?"

"You said drugs and alcohol were commonplace with the band. Are you going back to that lifestyle? How will you be able to stay sober?"

Nikki threw her hands up to cover her mouth and shook her head. "I hadn't thought that far ahead. I've just been basking in the moment…I don't know what to do… Singing is my life…"

Nikki's phone rang then she looked at the caller ID, which showed it came from Neil. "Think I should take this call."

As Nikki walked away, her mom whispered, "Dear Lord, guide and direct my daughter to make the right decision."

Chapter 15

There was a whirl of activity at the inn the next several days as a family had booked all the rooms for a holiday reunion. They'd scheduled this family gathering there for the last five years, but this was the first time Nikki was there to assist her mother, who greatly appreciated the additional pair of hands. Nikki remembered the many times her mom helped and encouraged her. Now she could pay that back.

She was proud of her mom for continuing to make a success of the inn even after her dad had died. It was a lot of work for one person and there wasn't much of a profit margin to add additional employees. But she rarely heard her mom complain. Instead, she'd say, "Tony is up there watching over me and encouraging me. In my heart, I still feel we're running it like a team."

When it was time for Nikki to pick up food items for the inn from Kayla's coffee shop, she was glad for the opportunity to catch up with her friend. Breezing into the coffee shop, she stopped and exclaimed, "This has got to be what heaven will smell like."

Several of the customers smiled along with Kayla as Nikki made her way to the counter. "Give me your special of the day and my favorite blend of Chai tea. And make sure I don't forget to pick up all the stuff for my mom before I leave."

"Michael seems a bit cheerier lately. Are you the reason for that?" Kayla asked as she filled Nikki's order.

Nikki's eyes brightened. "Yes, I've been spending time with Michael helping with his rehearsals. He's so amazing with those kids.

Did you know he's even writing songs again?"

"Really? He's redone arrangements for some songs we sing, but I didn't know he was creating new ones. What are they like?"

Nikki sipped her tea and took a nibble at her cranberry orange crumble muffin. "This is so good, but back to Michael. When he wrote country songs, they told a story. Now the stories are about God. His faith shines through when he sings them. They've even brought tears to my eyes for their poignancy."

"Wow. When does he plan to play them at church?"

"He says he's still working on them, but he gets this little twinkle in his eye as if he's got a secret he doesn't want to share."

"If Luke knew something about the music, I'd think he would have mentioned it to me. Unless it's a secret between them."

"The songs would do well on record charts and sales. I've got a strong instinct about what's hit worthy or not. These could be chart toppers. Does the church produce music to sell?"

"No, it's just the online videos for our church services and special events."

Kayla filled orders for a couple of customers before returning to Nikki again. "Since things seemed to be warming up between you and Michael, are you going to be staying on after the holidays?"

Nikki swirled the remaining tea in her cup, then shrugged. "I'm going to be here through Christmas, but the band is getting together to be part of this huge New Year's Eve bash. It'll be the first time we play together since Neil's rehab. It's a pretty big thing and I need to be there as well."

"Are they playing in one of the New York Times Square events?"

"A bit further away. We'll be playing at the Southbank Centre in London."

"And then what?" Kayla thrust her hands on the counter and frowned at Nikki. "Are you going back on tour? And I'll see you again in maybe another three years? I thought you needed a break from the band?"

"I did. I've enjoyed being back in town and spending time with Michael. But I'm a singer, that's what I do. Singers go on tour. I'm not sure what's next for the band, but I'm doing this event. The money is good, and I'd be a fool not to be there."

"Have you told Michael yet?"

"No, I made the decision last night. You're the first one I've told."

"So, it's going to be like last time when you left. You'll break Michael's heart again."

"No, it's not like that."

"That show, *America's Next Best Talent* was only going to be a one-time thing. Then you got the gig with Neil and the band. Off you went without looking back. Sure, we all cheered you on and wished you the best, but you said goodbye to Michael with a text like he was a fan."

145

"I was blown away by having my dream come true. Everything was so new and exciting. I couldn't focus on anything else."

"It looks to me like you're doing it again. This time make sure you actually talk to Michael. If you still want to have something special with him, let him know. If not, tell him. Now, I need to put some more pastries in the oven. I'll get the items your mom ordered and bring them out to you."

Without waiting for Nikki to respond, Kayla turned away. Nikki glared at Kayla's turned back for a moment then sighed and nodded. Kayla was right. She owed it to Michael to tell him how she felt and why she was taking this gig. Michael had his music, and she had her career. Singing was her life, and she wasn't going to give that up. *God, help me find the right words to say, so I don't hurt Michael again.*

Chapter 16

For the next several days, Nikki had little time to think about what would happen after Christmas. She was too busy helping her mom serve meals, assisting with afternoon happy hours, and setting up events for the extended family staying at the inn. During her midmorning breaks she read the Bible and prayed.

As suggested by the AA program, she went to daily meetings, mostly in the afternoons so she could be at the evening rehearsals with Michael. In addition, she found other AA members she could count on to help her with her sobriety. Darlene, who had been in the program for 10 years, became her sponsor. She liked the woman and appreciated the way she walked her through the steps of the program. Darlene was easy to confide in and didn't accept any excuses or whining. The other reason Nikki chose her was the fact the woman was also a Christian and said she was praying for her.

When Wednesday evening rolled around, Nikki was off for the rehearsal with Michael and the teens. She was looking forward to it and dreading it at the same time. A couple of weeks ago, the dreading part would have been having to listen to the Christian songs. Now it was the music she enjoyed most, and she listened to on the way to the church. The hard part she dreaded was telling Michael that she was leaving again.

She couldn't give him any assurances she'd come back after the gig because singing with the band was like breathing air for her. She craved the excitement of seeing and hearing all the fans. The off time was the problem. When the band wasn't on stage, it was anything goes, and they did whatever they pleased. If she and Neil could be a support team for the sake of their sobriety and separate themselves from the rowdiness, she could stay with the band. When they had breaks from the tours she'd come home to Culver Creek. It was a long shot, but she hoped it would work so she could have her career and a relationship with Michael.

As she walked through the church doors she prayed silently, *Jesus, help me to find the right words to say to Michael. I want a second chance at love with him and I want to keep singing. Let me know what it is you want me to do with my life. Please make it clear to me. Amen.*

Shrieks of delight rose to her ears as some of the female teens noticed her arrival.

"Look it's Nicole!"

"You're back again."

"I've been practicing like you suggested."

"Wait until you hear me."

She placed a hand to her heart and bowed. Turning to Michael and seeing him filled her with a happiness that made her feel as if all her worries and stresses had melted away. A smile flashed across his face in return as she hastened her steps toward the front of the church where they would be practicing this evening. She dropped her coat and gloves on one of the nearby chairs and put her hands on her hips. "What songs will we be singing tonight to raise a joyful noise to the Lord?"

A cacophony of answers erupted with multiple voices chiming in with their favorite songs. Michael raised his hand to quiet everyone. "Yes, those are all the songs. Now let's go through them one by one. We will begin with "What Child is This" and sing it through one stanza at a time. Nicole and I will make suggestions as needed."

They went through each song in a similar manner with each vocal chorus improving over the previous one. At what seemed to be the end of the rehearsal, Michael began to play random notes on the piano as he spoke. "Now my gifted vocalists, it's time to make the decision about a special song to end our program. You know I haven't picked anyone yet to sing "O Holy Night" with the chorus in the background. There's still one person I've yet to audition for that part…Raise your hands if you want me to have Nicole audition."

To no great surprise, the majority of students raised their hands with the exception of the few who had hoped to do the final solo themselves. "Good, we have a majority who want you to audition. Here's the sheet music, Nicole. Follow along as the group sings it for you."

"But Michael don't – "

Michael raised a hand to stop Nicole from continuing. "Please follow along. As you can see, the music is in the key that works best for you. I don't expect it to be perfect the first time as you're not familiar with my arrangement.

Now is everyone else ready?"

The teens straightened their posture and nodded, then Michael started the intro, and the singers began. Nicole had heard the song on the radio and as background music in stores during Christmas. Michael's piano accompaniment and the chorus stirred a sense of joy in her heart. When the song was over, she had a lump in her throat and applauded. Her voice cracked as she replied, "I'm awed. That was beautiful."

"It's one of my favorites," Michael replied. "Are you ready to give it a go?"

"Help me along by singing it with me."

"Okay, let's do this duet style. I'll sing the first stanza, you do the second, in the third we'll sing together. Then we'll start again with you alone."

Nicole nodded and Michael began playing.

Once they ran through the three stanzas, The teens broke out with enthusiastic applause and cheers.

"Wow. That was great."

"Do the song as a duet."

And that led into the chant, "Duet. Duet. Duet. Duet."

Michael and Nicole stared at each other dumbfounded. That wasn't the reaction Michael expected, but he liked it. "Are you really sure you want the two of us to do the song together with the chorus in the background?"

Applause and cheers resounded again.

Michael quieted everyone. "Okay. We'll do it. But I want a dynamic chorus to back up our duet. This will be our grand finale. I want this song to truly touch the hearts of those listening."

Nicole waited until the rehearsal was over, and all the kids left. There was no delaying it. Now was the time she needed to tell Michael that she would be leaving after Christmas to do a show in London.

Michael noticed the change in her posture and how her smile had diminished. "You look kind of serious. Is there something wrong?"

Nikki took a deep breath as her mind raced like the twists and turns of a roller coaster trying to figure out what to say next. "I need to tell you something. First off, I'm excited about doing the song with you. It's so moving. And I love working with the kids. It's going to be a great show."

Her mouth felt dry as a cotton ball, but she continued on. "What I tell you next, may make you not want to keep me in the program at all… I'm leaving right after Christmas. I'm heading back to the band. We'll be rehearsing for our gig on New Year's Eve in London. It's a really big bash. Parts of it will even be on TV. It's a great opportunity. I really can't pass it up."

Michael's shoulders slumped. He shook his head and sighed as he turned away from Nicole. "I can't believe this is happening again. But at least this isn't your goodbye in a text message. Guess I should be grateful for that." He turned to face her. Disappointment iced his words as he spoke just above a whisper. "I thought we were moving toward a relationship together, but you're still running off to chase your dreams of stardom. That seems to be what is most important to you."

Nicole reached for his hands and held them tight. "No, it's not like that. This is just one gig. I don't know what else they have lined up, but I'll probably come right back here until the next tour is set up."

Michael pulled away and stood on the other side of the piano. "That's what you said about the talent show. This event will lead to other gigs like back then. And what are your plans about your sobriety? How will you deal with that being around the band?"

"You've told me there are AA groups around the world. I'll find some in London. I'll go to meetings. And I can call my sponsor for more support."

Michael raised an eyebrow. "Sounds like you've thought this through and are ready to go."

"Yes, Michael." Nicole tugged at her hair. "You know how much I love singing. This is something I need to do. I'll come back. You'll see."

"I know you need to do it, but I don't think you're even sure where it's going to end." He blew out a deep breath as his hands clenched the top edge of the piano. "I wish you the best.

As far as working with the Christmas program… well, we're both professionals and will function as such for the good of the show and the church. So, yes, I want you to continue with us. I have a busy day tomorrow, so let me lock up. I'll see you at the next rehearsal."

Nicole's body felt glued in place but in her mind, she wanted to jump up and down and scream, "No, don't write me off like that. It's not fair." Instead, she nodded imperceptibly as he headed toward the church's main doors. Feeling as if she was in a trance, she followed him robotically with her head hung low.

As he held the door open for her, Nicole hoped he would say that he understood and would wait for her return. But all he said was "Drive safe," before he turned and locked the door.

As she ran down the church steps a gust of wind whipped away her first tears but did nothing to prevent the coming rush of more of them.

Chapter 17

When Nikki arrived home, she was thankful that her mother had already gone to bed. Feeling like her life had been torn out from under her, she quietly searched the kitchen cabinets for her mom's bottle of good cognac. Then she dropped a couple of ice cubes in the glass and poured in a heavy dose of the alcohol. She brought the glass up to her lips that would numb her feelings. But then held it there without letting the numbing elixir roll over her tongue.

Her hand shook as she brought the glass down to the counter and stared at the drink. Without hesitation, she rummaged through her purse for her cell phone. She hit the number for her sponsor and hoped she'd pick up the call even though it was 11:00 o'clock.

Darlene picked up on the third ring and having noticed the caller ID immediately said, "What's the problem, Nikki? How can I help you?"

"I want a drink, but I don't want to take a drink. I don't want to start that cycle again. I poured a drink and it's sitting in front of me."

"Where are you?"

"At home."

"If you want to maintain your sobriety, throw that drink down the drain. Don't hesitate. Have you done it?"

Nikki dumped the drink into the sink and put the bottle away.

"What happened that threw you off?"

Nikki sobbed. "I made a mess of things, again."

"Have you been drinking?"

Nikki shook her head and then realized she had to vocalize the thought and did.

"Good. What I want you to do is pick up your keys and come over to my place so we can talk this out without the temptation of a bottle near you."

After getting directions, Nikki picked up her keys, rushed to the door, and softly locked it behind her. Her destination was a small motel located near the state highway where her sponsor worked. Pulling into the lot, she saw Darlene sitting at the front desk waving to her through the large window framed by blinking colored lights.

Parking the car as close as possible to the door, Nikki pulled her collar up and stuck her hands into her pockets as she hastened to the lobby entrance. Giving her sponsor a quick hug she added, "Thanks for letting me come see you."

"Not a problem, that's what a sponsor is for. I'm doing the first part of the night shift until 1:00
a.m. so it's easy to do. Have a seat."

Nikki sat in the brown and yellow plaid cushioned chair beside Darlene. The table between them had brochures touting fun things to do nearby. A Christmas tree stood a few feet away that was decorated with gold and silver ornaments and topped with a twinkling gold star emblazoned with the motel's name. In the background, soft instrumental Christmas songs played. The cozy feel of the room put her at ease.

"What happened today that made you want to reach for a drink?"

Nikki laughed nervously. "You don't waste time do you, so I'll get to the point. Tonight I told my ex-boyfriend from years back, who I thought was becoming my new boyfriend, I was leaving right after Christmas to go to London for a gig on New Year's Eve. He called me out for sabotaging our relationship, again."

A raised eyebrow and a nod let Nikki know she should continue. Much of what she said seemed like she was babbling as she fidgeted in the chair or tugged at her hair, but she was trying to process her feelings as she spoke. When she finished, she slumped back into the chair and let out a deep sigh.

Darlene leaned forward and patted Nikki's knee. "You've done a good job with AA's first three steps. You admitted you were powerless over alcohol and your life had become unmanageable. You believe a Power greater than yourself could restore you to sanity. And you've shown you're willing to turn your will and your life over to the care of God.

But you haven't done your fourth step yet. People reach for a fifth because they didn't do the fourth step. They don't have a coping mechanism other than alcohol to deal with the guilt and shame. That's something you need to work on now.

Darlene got up, opened a drawer behind the front desk, and pulled out a legal-size lined notepad and a couple of pens, which she brought over to Nikki. "Step four is 'Made a searching and fearless moral inventory of ourselves and our wrongs.' That's what I want you to do. Start writing and don't stop until you've finished."

Nikki grimaced at the suggestion, but seeing Darlene wasn't offering any other options, she began to write. The writing continued with starts and stops to when the next shift manager came into the lobby.

Darlene directed Nikki to the apartment behind the office and closed the door behind them. "Take all the time you need to write your heart out. I'll be in the next room napping. When you're done, come wake me and we'll do the fifth step."

While Darlene slept, Nikki continued to grapple with the mistakes she made and how she had wronged others in the process. Owning up to her lies and deceptions to herself and others was hard to do, but she knew this was necessary to move forward and make her life better. When she finally finished writing, she stretched out her fingers and flexed them for a few seconds, then rubbed her neck.

Closing her eyes she relaxed as snippets from a Christian song she'd heard recently flitted through her mind. The lyrics told about giving your burdens, shame, and hurts to Jesus…not waiting until you were perfect… just to come with an open heart seeking forgiveness.

She put her elbows on the table and folded her hands and silently prayed. *Jesus, I'm not very experienced at this prayer thing. Forgive me for all the hurtful, uncaring stuff I've done. Help me to do better to make up for all my wrongs. Help me see what you want me to do with my life.*

When she called Darlene back into the room, the woman listened to Nikki's long list of wrongs without reproach. That gave Nikki the courage to continue in her honest self-assessment and to seek forgiveness -- first from God and then from others. Declaring it was a bit disconcerting but freeing at the same time. Through it all she had a sense of peace knowing she was on the right path. Starting tomorrow, well actually later that day, she'd start finding ways to make amends.

Chapter 18

The next two weeks of Nikki's life flew by in a whirlwind of emotions, each day blending into the next as if time itself was healing old wounds. One of the most heartfelt amends she needed to make was to her mother, whom she had abandoned after her father's death, immersing herself in her career and thinking of no one else.

Now, Nikki found joy in spending time at the inn, doing whatever she could to ease her mother's burdens. Whether it was preparing breakfast for guests or running errands, she embraced every task with a newfound purpose. Often, she'd pause to admire her mother's quiet strength, her eyes welling up with a mix of admiration and regret for time lost. "You've always been an incredible role model," she would say, her voice trembling with sincerity. Each compliment was a small but significant step toward mending their fractured bond, and for the first time in years, Nikki truly felt the warmth of being home.

The other amends she needed to make were to her old friends for the caustic remarks she had hurled during her drunken rant. Each apology was filled with nerves and remorse as she faced them one by one.

To her surprise, rekindling those friendships felt like coming home. As they laughed, joked, and reminisced about their teen years and shared hopes for the future, she marveled at the warmth of their acceptance.

Her heart swelled with a mix of gratitude and regret for the lost time. This time when she left, she'd keep those bonds strong and not let their relationships together slip away again.

Unfortunately, it wasn't that easy with Michael. An impenetrable wall had come between them since the night she told him of her upcoming departure. He wasn't mean or dismissive but their relationship had become a strictly professional one that only existed at the rehearsals. He didn't attend any of the same AA meetings she did. And in her meetings with old friends he would be absent. Usually during rehearsals she'd see the look of sadness as he glanced in her direction, then quickly turn away.

When Nikki dropped in to Kayla's coffee shop the day of the Christmas program, she could tell that Kayla was still upset with her. But at least they were still talking. She deliberately waited until there was a break of customers so the two of them could talk.

"Tonight the big night. Can't believe I'm just as nervous for this event as I've been when starting my big concerts." Nikki nervously tapped her fingers on the counter. "You'd think it would be easier, but these people know me, and I don't want to disappoint them."

Kayla rolled her eyes as she leaned on the counter facing her friend. "Really, Nikki? You know this concert isn't about you. It's about celebrating the birth of Christ."

Nikki shook her head. "No, I didn't mean to imply that at all. It's just that doing this concert makes me feel like I'm a teenager again. Not an adult. It's the last thing I expected I'd be doing when I came back. And I'm glad I am doing it. Because of Michael I've been able to make some big changes in my life. Due to his intervention, I've become sober and have a relationship with Jesus. I am totally grateful for that."

"But you're still leaving."

"Yes, I am a singer. I'm returning to my band. I want to see if this can still work for me. I don't want to have any "what ifs" in the back of my mind if I don't go. My sobriety and faith are my priorities. I also want to make it a commitment to come home as often as touring allows."

"Hate to say it Nikki but that sounds like the same old story you had after you started with Lockwood and Sutton. Why do you think it will be different now?"

"Because I'm a different person." Nikki reached for Kayla's hand and gripped it. Would you do me a big favor? Would you pray for me? Pray that I'll keep my sobriety and not lose my new found faith?"

Kayla smiled. "You know I will. I'll be praying that God will direct and guide you and keep you on the right path. And I'll be there tonight to cheer you and the kids as you sing. Looking forward to hearing your duet with Michael."

After a quick hug, Nicole headed out of the shop. Before going home she stopped at the local bookstore and picked up a yearly woman's devotional for her mom and one for herself to keep them connected. As she walked back to her car, she wiped away a tear falling down her cheek. She was gonna miss this town and her friends, but most importantly -- Michael.

It felt bittersweet as Nikki prepped for the evening's performance. Memories of the past performances she had done in the town with Michael flooded her memory. Would they ever regain what they once had? She wasn't ready to leave the thrill of playing before thousands of excited fans and just play for a local club or two.

There had to be a way to make it work -- to still tour with the band and come back to her hometown between shows. But Michael was afraid of getting his heart broken again and she didn't know how to rebuild his trust in her.

She carefully folded her bagged dress for the evening's performance over her arm. Adding her coat and purse to her other hand, she headed toward the apartment's kitchen.

Her bags were already packed for the trip to London the next day. But tonight she wouldn't think about that. She'd appreciate every second of this evening and what her life had become in the month she had been home.

When her mom saw her walk into the room her eyes glistened. "I am so thrilled to know you're in the Christmas performance tonight. I think I'm as excited as you are. What a wonderful Christmas blessing." Her mom took the dress bag and hung it on a hook at the top of the kitchen door over her apron and gave Nikki a hug.

Then Nikki noticed her mother's smile sag. "Now don't start thinking about tomorrow. I promise I'll call you the day after the show. If the band doesn't surprise me with another gig that's set up, I'll be returning a day or so later." "Yes, honey, I understand. I'll be praying God will direct you to the plan he has for your life, and you'll have peace with it. Now sit and have a sandwich with me. With the dress rehearsal and practice, there will be little time to eat until after the show."

When Nikki arrived at the church, all the snow from the previous night had been cleared to the far section of the parking lot allowing plenty of room for cars. From the excess snow, someone had crafted a snow creche with Mary, Joseph, and Jesus.

Staring at the stars twinkling above her she pondered what it must have been like in Bethlehem over 2000 years ago when Mary and Joseph gave birth to their first son. Knowing the baby was no ordinary infant must have had Mary's mind in a whirl for being part of that glorious event.

Tonight they'd be celebrating that event which filled Nikki with joy. She pulled out her phone and took a picture for a special memory. *I wonder who did that? I'll ask Michael.* Her pulse quickened, knowing that for the next few hours she'd be with him even though she'd be sharing him with all the other singers.

Pulling her coat collar up to cover her ears, she scurried to the church's side door that led to the choir room. As her heels clicked walking down the hall, sounds of musicians tuning their instruments and anxious chatter filled the air.

Michael turned her way as she entered the room and seeing his smile made her heart skip a beat. There was so much she wanted to say to him before she left, but there was no time now. She'd need to find the time after the show. *Please dear God let us have that time to talk. I need to mend our relationship as best I can before leaving.*

The practice and dress rehearsal had only a few minor issues with the nervousness being replaced with joy and confidence under Michael's adept direction. He ended the rehearsal by calling everyone together for prayer. "Heavenly Father be with us tonight as we glorify your name. Let our voices ring clear and the music sound sweet. May the messages in the songs touch the hearts and minds of those in the audience. Bless and guide all those who have provided their time and talents to make this program a success. Amen."

Then everyone took their places on the stage or in the wings waiting for their time to cross over onto the stage. While Nikki waited for her song, she encouraged the other singers with applause and thumbs up movements. She wouldn't be singing for thousands tonight, but singing for family and friends filled her with contentment unmatched by her shows with Lockwood & Sutton.

When the program neared its end, the stage lights dimmed leaving only shadowed spotlights on the actors playing the Holy Family, shepherds, and wise men. A brighter spotlight glowed around Michael as he played the intro to their song on the piano.

Nikki stepped beside the piano facing Michael and the audience. As they sang alternating verses for "O Holy Night," she wished the song could go on forever as the words filled her heart with the love of God and the joy of singing with Michael. Too soon the song ended, and everyone was taking their bows amidst resounding whistles and applause.

After the show, family and friends gathered around the performers to offer their congratulations. While Nikki chatted with them, her eyes kept wandering toward Michael, her heart aching to be alone with him. Finally, when the crowd had thinned, she hurriedly made her move over to Michael and whispered, "Let's go for a walk."

She noticed the hesitation in his eyes and squeezed his hand. "Please… I need you to hear me out before I leave."

He nodded but his eyes still had a questioning look about them as if he were

176

stealing himself against some emotional hurt he expected from her.

They walked toward the choir room in silence and found it was deserted. Nikki took his hand and stepped over to a small table with two upholstered chairs. Taking both his hands in hers she gulped down a lump in her throat and quickly prayed a silent prayer before she began. "Michael, you know how much these last few weeks have meant to me. When I first came home, I felt like a zombie, but you brought me to life again and gave me a new hope."

Tears began to well in her eyes, but she continued. You showed me the way to get sober and brought me to a relationship with Jesus. And I feel… that we have a second chance at love."

"It's a second chance for you to leave again." Michael tried to pull away, but Nikki held tightly to his hands.

"This time it will only be for a week at most."

"Really? You think that the band's not lining up other gigs to make up for the loss of two months' income?"

"I don't know. Maybe. I've got to do this gig. I really love singing with the band. They're my friends. I'm hoping Neil's stint in drug rehab will create a positive change for the band, but I don't know what to expect. I can't and I won't go back to a life of drugs and drinking. Will you pray that I won't lose my sobriety as a result of being with them again? Will you pray that my faith will continue to strengthen?"

Michael had been avoiding her gaze but now he stared deeply into her eyes as if trying to see the future. "Of course, I will. Nicole, I know how much your singing career means to you, but there are other options. You'll be able to see them once you make a clean break from the band. I'll pray for you, but I won't put my life on hold for you again."

Nikki threw her arms around Michael. "You won't have to. I don't want to lose you again. I will come back, very soon. I promise."

"I don't wanna lose you again either. I've been writing more songs and when you return, I'll share what I'm doing with them."

Nikki pulled away from the embrace and gave him a quick kiss. "That's wonderful Michael. I can't wait to hear them."

Michael pulled her closer, his lips brushing hers in a gentle kiss. Then, as if imprinting the moment into their hearts, they kissed again, this time with a fervent intensity, as if desperate to make the memory last until they would be together again.

Chapter 19

Even with the luxury of a first-class ticket to London, Nikki was still anxious and uncertain. Holding to her conviction of keeping her sobriety, she declined the free alcoholic drinks available. Throughout the flight, her mind was bouncing around like a ping pong ball wondering what it would be like with the band. Would her band mates cut back on their drinking and drugs to make it easier for her and Neil? Or would there be the normal excesses?

Would she fall into those old habits as well?

Since her arrival came in the early morning hours, she knew no one would be there to meet her. Band members rarely got up before noon. No problem. The first order of business was to attend an AA meeting. She had already downloaded a meeting guide on her phone. There were options for both online and in person meetings. She chose a location that was not too far from her hotel. Although her room wasn't ready yet, she was able to leave her bags with the front desk personnel in a secure area.

A short cab ride brought her to a church which provided a side room for their meeting. The directions on her app even gave her details as to where to enter the church and find the room. Hearing chatter and laughter as she walked down the hall, put her at ease. She had a feeling there would be the same camaraderie that existed at her hometown meetings.

When she was greeted at the door and saw others holding AA 12 step books, she felt her shoulders relax. At the point of the meeting where the speaker asked if there were any visitors, she raised her hand and stood up with a few others in the room. When it was her turn to speak, she smiled and looked around the room. "Hello all, my name is Nicole. I'm visiting here from the US and have been sober for 23 days." In return, those in the room replied, "Welcome" and applauded. Once she sat, the woman seated next to her leaned over and whispered, "Keep coming back, lass. Soon you'll be getting your 30 day chip. I've been sober for five years now. Best decision I ever made."

"My best decision, too." Nikki whispered back.

The step they were covering in the meeting was Step 6 which is "Were entirely ready to have God remove all these defects of character." Nikki listened as the step and the first paragraph in the book was read. She shook her head. *Am I really ready to be honest about all my defects in character? Oh sure, I could glibly say that I was, but would it be true? I don't think so. All my defects removed sounds like a tall order, but I know my fellow AA members would tell me that God could indeed do that. It just comes down to my own willingness.*

Both Michael and Kayla have pointed out to me that I am obsessed with fame. That I like to say I'm a part of a hugely popular band. What's wrong with that? I love singing. I love the adrenaline rush. And the money. But who would I be if the band split up? Is that all I am?

Michael had it all - the fame and the money. But he gave it up and said he found something more fulfilling. I can see that's true in the way he interacts with his teens and the excitement he shows playing music and writing new songs.

But what about me? Could I be satisfied just singing songs at the church or at small local venues?

Her thoughts were interrupted upon hearing one of the other AA members make a comment after reading a paragraph in the step study.

"You know I used to think it was all about me. The big #1. The star. I had money to burn. The fancy cars. The custom tailored clothes. Front row seats at shows. I was tops in my sales field. But nothing really satisfied me. I started drinking to push away that inadequacy. But then drinking became the big #1 before I even realized it.

Now I mentor a small group of entrepreneurs who want to start their own businesses and I point them to the importance of helping others as well. It's pure satisfaction when I see them succeed. Do I still have character defects? Ask my wife. She'll tell you I still procrastinate about doing chores around the house. But I'm striving to do better."

Whoa! Nikki thought. *Thinking it is all about me is certainly self-centered. That's a big defect of character I need to work on. Okay, God, that got my attention. I certainly*

184

need to strive to do better. You gave me the talent to sing. Let me nurture that talent so it's more than just getting accolades for myself. Let me remember to praise you even more so. Maybe I can talk to the guys in the band about supporting some charities in the communities where we do concerts.

After the meeting Nikki stayed around for several minutes to chat with the locals to see what suggestions they had for other meetings during the day and late at night after concerts. However she still kept her anonymity and didn't mention she was in a band. It really didn't matter as no one would recognize her anyway since she wasn't sporting her signature multicolored hair. That's something she would have to fix before they played the New Year's Eve bash.

Before heading back to her hotel, she stopped at a local coffee shop and got a Chai latte. While shipping the drink, she scanned the Internet to find a wigmaker who could create her signature look without having to dye her own hair again. Once that task was completed, she sent short text messages to her mom and Kayla.

> No issues with the flight.
> Arrived on time. Went to AA
> meeting. Having snack now.
> Taking a nap is next before
> afternoon rehearsal that could
> last hours into the night. Miss
> you.

Then she took a selfie holding the mug of tea in her other hand and sent it to Michael with a more personal text message.

> Arrived safely in London.
> Having a proper cup of tea.
> Went to 6th step study meeting.
> Realized one of my character
> defects is thinking that
> everything's about me and
> music. Got to add more action
> to my life. Share my blessings
> with others. When I return, we'll

have to discuss those "other options" for my singing that you alluded to before I left. Love you and miss you.

A short nap back at the hotel refreshed Nikki. Adrenaline started kicking in she dressed to meet her bandmates and she began softly singing some of her favorite band songs. She had missed them and realized how excited she was to see them again. The cab ride to the rehearsal studio seemed to take forever when in reality it was only about 25 minutes.

There were cheers, hugs, and kisses all around when she entered the studio. Her eyes bugged out on seeing the radical change in Neil's appearance. His skin had a healthy color, and his eyes were clear and bright. He looked every inch like the attractive, muscled, and well-dressed talent judge she'd met years earlier.

She gave him a joyful hug. "Rehab looks fantastic on you. Your decision made me rethink my choices as well. I don't have six weeks sobriety like you, but I do have a little over three weeks."

Neil hugged her again. "That's wonderful luv." Holding her close he whistled to get everyone's attention. "I'm not the only sober member of the band now, Nikki's taken the no drinking pledge as well."

The applause they received included cheers from the other band members who held up their glasses or bottles of alcohol.

"All right lads and lasses let's get down to business and practice. I wrote a new song while in rehab. I'd like to try it out to see if we could include it. Now before you wonder who the old flame is in this song, let me dispel any rumors. It's about my love for playing music. Here's how it goes."

Neil sat down at the piano and played the opening bars while the others listened where they sat or stood. "Our love story is not over yet. Despite distance and time, I can't forget. The love we shared when it was new, has stayed with me forever true..."

As Nikki listened to the song, her thoughts drifted to Michael and images of their being together. *I'm not gonna mess up our second chance at love. I'll call him once rehearsal is over.*

Everyone agreed they should include the song if they could get the right mix to make it work. The rest of the rehearsal ran smoothly with everyone feeling energized to be playing together again. When they finished at 10:00 p.m., she passed on going for drinks and a bite to eat saying she wanted to make a phone call.

That brought on an onslaught of comments. "Who's the new luv?" "No time wasted for you, pet." "How many are in your favorites phone list?" "Have you already scored a new luv in London?"

Heat rushed to her face as she shook her head and giggled. "Not a new luv, but an old one we're trying to rekindle. Now go off to your favorite pub while I return to my hotel by myself and make a phone call."

She fidgeted the whole time in the cab ride back to the hotel. She could have called while in the back seat, but she wanted to be able to curl up on the bed backed up by a bunch of pillows to make the call just like she did when they were teenagers and chatted before going to bed.

Unfortunately, there'd be no reminiscing of earlier times together that night. After several rings, the call went to voicemail, so she left a message. "I miss you, Michael. Wish you were available to talk. We just finished our first rehearsal and it went great.

Neil wrote a new song while in rehab that we'll be adding at our gig. It's a song about old love that's still new. Like us. I'll call you again tomorrow. Going to get an early night's sleep to get past jet lag. Love you. Can't wait to see you again."

Chapter 20

The next few days of rehearsals had their issues of clashing opinions, but in the end, they got the mix right and were ready to hit the stage for the New Year's Eve revelers. Once again, Nikki had her multi-colored hair, but this time it was a wig. Both her and Macie, the other female singer, wore short sequined dresses and numerous bangle bracelets that would glisten in the lights with every move they made.

The strobe lights flashed around the audience and then focused on the band as they walked onto the stage to sing their first song. The intoxicating rush of adrenaline from the roar of the crowd zigzagged through Nikki's body making her feel on top of the world. Hearing the fans sing along with them was the part of being a singer she adored. The heat of the lights plus the energy expended with dance moves and harmonies left her like a rag doll by the end of the evening, but she couldn't stop grinning.

Two encores had her head spinning with delight. This is what she loved and was enthralled by the idea of doing it again as soon as possible. It was totally intoxicating. But like the explosive bursts of sparkling colors and the crack and boom of the fireworks being launched, they end with a fizzle of smoke.

Her excitement quickly deflated with the next turn of events on stage. Her mouth dropped open and everything seemed to move in slow motion as she stood watching.

Bottles of champagne were brought on by members of their crew. They popped them open and sprayed the crowd and band members with foaming liquid. Band members sprayed each other or guzzled the champagne. It became a free-for-all that everyone seemed to enjoy except her. It brought back memories of drunken nights with the band and waking up with splitting headaches.

The once dazzling night had now lost its glitter. The scent of the sticky liquid dripping off her hair and body almost made her want to gag. This type of fun and play was something she no longer wanted to be a part of. A smile remained plastered on her face until the lights went out and then it disappeared as she walked off the stage.

While her other band members retreated to the musicians' lounge to drink some more and revel in the excitement of being on stage, Nikki went to the dressing room to change into street clothes. There wasn't any place to shower, but at least she could wash her face and arms and towel dry her wig and hair.

When she returned to the crowded lounge, she slipped over to where Neil was chatting with one of his groupies. She whispered in his ear, "I can't do this. I don't wanna lose my sobriety. I'll talk to you in the morning. Watch yourself."

Neil swirled the liquid in the glass he held. "Just soda water so I'm good. See you tomorrow, luv."

Nikki gave him a quick peck on the cheek and slipped out of the room, her mind twisting with a mix of emotions. Her decision had been made and it felt like a seismic shift in her life.

The once vibrant allure of the rockstar lifestyle had lost its luster. It was time for her to go home. Leaving would be bittersweet, as she was surrendering a cherished chapter of her life, but she trusted that God had another extraordinary plan waiting for her.

Chapter 21

Nikki checked flight schedules as soon as she woke up the next morning. Her decision was to head out on the next flight available. There was no reason for her to continue to stay in London. Prior to leaving, she left a long text message for Neil.

> Had a great time playing with everyone again last night, but it's time for me to make an exit. Thanks for all you taught me about singing and the music biz. My sobriety is paramount to me and I can see there's way too much temptation to fall off the wagon by staying in the band.

Luv you guys, but it's time I start

a new chapter in my life. Music

will still play a big part in it.

The flight back home would be a long one due to a couple of stops along the way at connecting airports. That didn't matter so much since she knew she was going home. By the time she exited the plane at Lehigh International Airport, she was tired and irritable. Rather than rent a car and drive home, she had pre-hired a driver knowing the flight would be a lengthy one and she'd be exhausted,

Once they were on the road, she checked her phone and noticed the battery was almost dead. She sent texts to Kayla, and her mom about heading home, but as she tapped in the number to call Michael, the phone died. *How could I forget to charge my phone? I really needed to talk to Michael. Guess it will have to wait until I'm home.* Though she wrestled with the frustration for a few minutes, the movement of the car made her drowsy as jet lag took over. She closed her eyes and drifted off to sleep.

As she slept, she dreamed of being dressed like Dorothy Gale of Oz and gleefully running toward Michael and shouting, "There's no place like home. There's no place like home." But Michael's costume wasn't from a character in the Oz story. Instead, he wore a rhinestone cowboy suit and was singing about how he was gonna make it big in all the spotlights and was waving goodbye to her.

The dream disconcerted her enough that she awoke. *Now what in the world did that dream mean? Is he going to leave me for fame just like I once left him?*

While she was in London, she had only been able to leave text or voicemail messages for Michael. His responses were short and noncommittal. Was he just too busy to talk? Or was he holding his heart apart from her for fear it would be stepped on again?

Now she wondered if her dream had a real meaning to it. *Is my subconscious telling me I've lost my second chance? I pray that's not the case.* And pray was what she did silently until the car turned into the inn's parking lot.

Even before the driver removed her bags from the trunk, her mother was running out to meet her. After her mom held her in a deep hug, she pulled away and looked into Nikki's eyes. "Is this going to be another short layover at home? Or are you here for good?"

Nikki enthusiastically nodded as they embraced again. "Yes, that chapter of my life is over. I'm here to start a new one."

Once Nikki put her bags in her bedroom and attached her phone to a fast charger, she returned to the kitchen. While she enjoyed the tea and sweets she had in London, there was nothing like her mom's red velvet cinnamon rolls. She bit off a piece of the roll and closed her eyes for a moment savoring the sugary treat. "You absolutely make the best cinnamon rolls."

"Thanks. Do you want to rest up before tonight's party?"

"What party?"

Her mom gave her a quizzical look. "I thought that's the reason you came home. Tonight's Michael's birthday bash that Kayla put together."

Nikki smacked her hand against her forehead. "Arggh, my brain's a foggy mess from the London gig and traveling. I totally forgot about Michael's birthday. Wait. I don't even remember hearing about a party."

"Well, I think it was somewhat of a short notice thing. Kayla thought it might be a good idea to take Michael's mind off the fact that you were in London."

"I've got to be there." She pulled her hand through her hair and frowned. "What should I wear? What should I bring?"

"Now don't get in a tizzy. It's nothing fancy. Kayla reserved the private room at Sal's. She and some others spent last night putting all sorts of birthday decorations together to make him feel special. The dress is casual. You'll have no trouble finding something to wear."

"Right. Sure. Plenty of choices." Nikki took another bite of the cinnamon roll and a gulp of tea before rushing off to her room.

"You've got plenty of time." Her mom called after her. "Take a rest or a hot bath, so you don't fall asleep at the party."

Once in her room, Nikki began to pull things out of her closet, held them up to see how they looked in the mirror, and tossed what she didn't like on the bed – which was everything. Then she pulled out her special sweaters that were in plastic bags. That's where she found a teal V neck sweater with soft flowing sleeves dotted with little pearls that had a ruffled hem with a satin belt she could tie in a bow. It would go great with her blue jeans and black leather boots.

When jet lag had her yawning, she hastily returned all her clothes to the closet, set an alarm on her phone, which was still plugged into a charger, then flopped on her bed.

Forty-five minutes later, she awoke with an idea of what to bring to Michael's birthday party. She sorted through her memory box from high school and pulled out the playbill for "Dreamland" that showed her and Michael. She scanned that image and one of her duets with Michael at the Christmas show and added them to her computer.

With those pictures, other images, and text, she created a tri-fold mini poster showing their history together with her hope for their future. Satisfied with the finished product, she downloaded it to a thumb drive that she'd take to the Post and Print shop downtown.

After a quick shower and getting into clean clothes, Nikki picked up her coat and purse and headed to the kitchen.

"Well, you look refreshed. I'd offer you a snack, but it looks like you're on your way out," her mom said as she dried her hands on a towel. "Surprised you have plans already."

"Not really. Just bringing a mini poster design I made for Michael to get printed. I'll also look around for something special for him."

"Rather than gifts, Kayla asked people to bring canned and packaged food items for the church's food pantry. But I'm sure a few fun gifts will be brought as well."

"Okay, I'll pick up a few things at the supermarket. See you later."

After she dropped the thumb drive at the print shop, she headed to Memories and Dreams gift shop. There were wonderful gifts she could have personalized, but they wouldn't be ready the same day.

As she continued to peruse, she found a leather-bound journal with embossed musical notes on the cover that he could use to jot down lyrics and thoughts. Contented with the notebook, she took it to the cashier.

Next, she strode to Coffee Haven and Sweets. Kayla was swamped with customers, so she stood in line waiting her turn.

Once she reached the counter, Kayla gave Nikki a quick hug. "So, you've come back. And this time it's for good?"

Nikki nodded enthusiastically. "Yes, I'm here to stay. I've changed my life priorities, but the band didn't. I didn't fit in there anymore. This is where I belong."

"Does Michael know?"

"No, my mind's scattered from the trip. My phone died on the ride home and I left it at the inn before I came shopping for the party - which you didn't even tell me about."

Kayla shrugged. "Hearing how things were going with the band leading up to your New

Year's Eve show, I really didn't think you'd be heading home right after it. But I'm glad you did."

"Can I borrow your phone to call him?"

Kayla shook her head. "No. Let's make your appearance a great birthday surprise so you can see his joy in person."

Chapter 22

When Nikki and her mom arrived at the restaurant's private room, they were met with smiling faces and laughter. Streamers and balloons were festooned all around the walls. A side area designated for food pantry donations was already quite large. She placed her shopping bag of canned goods alongside the others.

The aroma of garlic, oregano, basil, and fresh bread wafted through the air. Her mom moved towards some friends who beckoned to her, While Nikki glanced around to see where Michael might be, she had no luck in finding him. Seeing Kayla waving to her, she walked that way. Pointing to the tables that already had some people at them, Nikki asked. "Is there assigned seating?"

"See the table mark reserved? That's for Michael, Luke, myself, the pastor, and his wife, and you."

"Thank you." Nikki hugged Kayla and held tightly to the gift bag for Michael. "I really need time to talk to him."

"That might be hard to do. Lots of people are here to celebrate with him. He's driving over with Luke. They'll be here soon."

A chorus of happy birthday immediately erupted when Michael walked in. He made his way through the crowd thanking them for coming but kept stealing glances her way. They drew closer. Nikki's heart beat faster and her mouth felt dry. How could she have ever left this man so many years ago?

Her thoughts cascaded with memories of tender moments from the past. The way his eyes looked deep into hers as if wanting to know everything about her. Whispers between romantic scenes in their musicals and saying this wasn't acting, but their real feelings. And after high school when they said their future would be making music together for the rest of their lives.

Just as their hands clasped, there was a whistle and a tap on the microphone to get everyone's attention. But Michael chose to ignore it as a grin filled his face and he whispered, "How are you even here? You're supposed to be in London. What happened?"

"I wanted to be here. Not in London. I wanted to be with you."

Before Michael could respond, Luke's voice came over the microphone. Okay everyone, find a seat. The only reserved ones are at the front table where Michael needs to come and take a seat now."

Michael gave an imploring look to Luke as he pointed to Nicole.

"Don't worry Michael, Nicole will be at the table with you. The two of you can chat later. We've got some people who would like to say a few words about you and your birthday celebration. So let's get this party started so the servers can bring in the food.

Michael put his arm around Nicole as they walked to the table And whispered in her ear. "Please don't leave until we get that time to talk."

Nicole whispered back. "You have nothing to worry about. I don't plan to leave. My time is your time tonight."

As the two of them sat and others found their places. Luke continued. "Tonight we're not only celebrating Michael's birthday but also what he's brought to the church as a musical director. You know, it's said you should play to your strengths. So how can Michael write inspiring Christian praise music, play a piano beautifully, strum a heartbreak country song, and encourage teens to actually study and learn their music. Come on dude, leave something for the rest of us."

"Giving sermons is way out of my league, so you have nothing to worry about," Michael quipped back.

After Luke shared additional comments on some of his experiences with Michael, he handed the microphone over to the head pastor, Dr. Jeremiah Clark.

"I've known Michael since he was a teenager and sang in our Christmas pageants. He certainly seemed talented then, But he's only improved as each birthday year has gone by. We're blessed for having him as part of our worship team and hope we'll have him with us for many years to come.

His songwriting talent is amazing. You might even say that every time Michael writes a country song about a love that's been lost, an angel loses its wings. But when he writes a praise song, the angel gets them back. It's a rollercoaster up there folks!"

While all the other guests ate, several of Michael's friends came to the microphone and expressed their sentiments of honoring Michael. Needing to pay attention to what they were saying prevented any discussion between him and Nicole.

He was grateful for what they had to say but he was extremely curious as to what was going on with Nicole. The only text he had received were those that expressed her joy of being back with the band and how good it felt.

Did she just come back for the party and plan on leaving again tomorrow? Or could it be possible that this time she wanted to stay? In between celebratory toasts he would glance her way and see her smile and feel her squeeze his hand. How he wished he could just stop time so the two of them could talk without any interruptions, but that would have to wait.

The comments continued and they filled his heart with joy…"Wishing a very Happy

Birthday to our musical director who makes learning new songs fun and inspiring!"

"Happy Birthday to the musician extraordinaire who plays music with one hand and touches hearts with the other!"

"Happy Birthday to the man who's a good friend, knows how to make us think with our hearts, laugh about our shortcomings that God can overcome, and point us to seek God, no matter what our circumstances!

When the speeches were finally over, Luke took the microphone again, "Now everyone raise your glass and wish happy birthday once more to Michael."

Applause followed as Michael stood and took the microphone from Luke. "Thank you one and all for coming tonight. This was a total surprise to me. All the wonderful words and funny stories you've told touch my heart. What a wonderful way to celebrate a birthday. Now go ahead and relax and enjoy your meal well I take a few minutes to chat with Nicole."

He handed the microphone back to Luke, then nodded to Nicole as he reached out his hand for her to follow him, so they could talk privately outside of this room. Since the restaurant was full, they had to settle for a quiet area in the hall. When he turned to face her, Nicole threw her arms around him and looked deep into his eyes.

"Oh, Michael, I'm so glad to be back home with you again. This is where I belong."

"But what about the band? Your texts made it seem like that was where you belonged?
What happened? Did the band break up?"

No. They're still going strong. I'm the one who left. I've no doubt they'll be able to find a new voice to replace mine easily enough. They're not gonna change. They're still all about the music, the booze and the parties. I'm the one who has changed. I can't do that anymore."

Michael lifted her chin. "Are you sure about that?" You won't miss the adrenaline rush playing for the crowds?"

"Yeah, I definitely enjoyed that, but I'm ready to start a new chapter in my life."
"Here?"

"Yes, here." She pulled him close. Their lips met in a soft, sweet kiss, tender and full of unspoken promises. It lingered just long enough to leave them both breathless. Then she leaned her forehead into his and whispered. "I should have never left you years ago. It was selfish and single minded of me. You were and are the best thing that ever happened to me. All those years ago when we sang about Dreamland, I didn't realize that being with you was my dream life, not my quest for the dream of fame. I want to be with you. Will you give us a second chance?"

"Are you sure you'll be happy in Culver Creek?"

"Yes, as long as we're together. You are my future wherever that might take me."

Michael pulled her close and their lips touched again, softly at first and then with more fervor. Nikki felt the beat of her heart matching his. This was where she was meant to be.

As they stood in the hallway, with their heads together, Michael whispered. "You know I've never stopped loving you even when we were apart. No one came close to what we had. No one ever will. I love you Nicole with all my heart.

Tears welled in Nikki's eyes. "I never stopped loving you either. I thought fame could fill my life, but I was so wrong. I want to be with you."

She handed him the gift bag that was a bit crunched up at this point. "This may seem a little silly, but I made a sort of birthday poster of our memories together. Music is what drew us together at the beginning and I want it to keep us together for many more birthdays to come. Do you have a place in the church chorus for me? I'm willing to audition."

As he looked at the pictures and text she had created, a deep smile spread across his face and his gaze turned to hers. "I don't want it to be just about music. I want it to be about our future together. This isn't the right time or place. I don't have a ring. We've known each other a long time. We've loved each other for a long time. I don't want to waste any more time. Will you marry me, Nicole?"

Once again, Nikki's eyes glistened with tears. "You really mean that? You want to marry me?"

Michael nodded and wrapped his arms around her.

Nikki whispered in his ear. "Then the answer is yes, for now, but I'm a romantic -- like the couples in sweet romance stories and movies. I still want the romantic down on one knee with a ring in hand that glistens in the light but not in the hallway of a restaurant."

Michael chuckled. "I'd be happy to do that and soon. Would a wedding after Easter and the music programs suit you?"

"Sounds like music to my ears." They kissed again with a joy that sent tingles throughout her body. She found her true love again and would never let him go.

Chapter 23

When Nikki left the band, she had no grand plans other than staying in Culver Creek and cherishing every moment with Michael. Yet each new day when she woke in the bedroom she grew up in, she felt a profound sense of joy and peace. Although unemployed, she found her days brimming with meaning and purpose.

The mornings started with helping her mom with daily chores at the inn. Their shared laughter and singing would occasionally echo through the halls as they rekindled their mother daughter bond. Her mother's patient, step-by-step instructions in meal preparation followed resolving the prior mystery of cooking.

Before this, Nikki's culinary repertoire was limited to making microwave popcorn and reheating restaurant leftovers while on tour with the band. Despite a few culinary mishaps, Nikki soon discovered a latent talent for cooking, her heart swelling with pride as she crafted new dishes from scratch.

But Nikki's transformation didn't stop in the kitchen. She embraced new routines, finding solace and strength in weekly AA meetings and spiritual nourishment in a ladies Bible study group. Her relationship with Michael deepened as they spent more quality time together.

Music remained a cornerstone of her life, and she joyfully immersed herself in the church's praise team, which Michael directed. Singing beside him, offering weekly praise to God, brought her an unparalleled sense of fulfillment. She often marveled at how wonderful her life had become, filled with unexpected blessings.

Then in a heartbeat, a few weeks later, everything shifted once more. It happened at the end of Abundant Life's Sunday service, during the final announcements made by Associate Pastor Luke Fletcher.

"We have been truly blessed with Michael Wilkerson's music ministry to this church," Luke began, his voice resonating through the sanctuary. "Before I give the final blessing and dismissal, he's got some news he'd like to share with you. C'mon over. Let everyone hear what you have to say."

As Michael moved to join Luke, he grasped Nikki's hand pulling her along with him.

A flicker of uncertainty crossed her face as she whispered, "What's this all about?"

Michael turned to her, his eyes twinkling with mischief and affection. He winked and squeezed her hand reassuringly. "Not to worry. You'll see."

The congregation watched in anticipation, the air thick with curiosity and excitement. Nikki's heart pounded, a mixture of exhilaration and nervousness swirling within her. What could Michael possibly have in store? She trusted him completely, and as she stood beside him, surrounded by their church family, she felt an overwhelming sense of gratitude and love. Whatever was about to happen, she knew it would be another beautiful chapter in their shared journey.

When the two of them faced the congregation, Michael's eyes sparkled with warmth as he began, "I'd like you to give a warm welcome to one of the newest members of our praise team. Of course, she's not a stranger to many of you, as you probably saw the two of us in musicals together in high school and singing at other community events over the years."

A wave of applause spread throughout the church, enveloping them in a comforting embrace. Michael raised one finger to signal for silence, his expression growing more earnest. "I'm truly blessed to have her as part of our praise team. She definitely adds something to the mix I felt I was missing in the band and my life."

Nikki's eyes welled up with tears of joy, her chest swelling with pride and love. The congregation's smiles and supportive nods made her feel an overwhelming sense of belonging and acceptance that was better than the rush of adrenaline she previously felt in playing with Lockwood and Sutton.

Michael continued, his voice filled with passion, "Today we played a new song that I wrote called, 'I Still Praise Him,' that I hope you liked. It's one of several others I've written that will be part of a new album published by Blessed Assurance Music Company. We'll start recording sessions in the next couple of weeks."

The applause grew louder, the congregation's enthusiasm echoing her own excitement. She squeezed Michael's hand, their fingers entwined in a silent promise of the beautiful future they would build together.

As applause erupted like a tidal wave, Michael leaned in close, his breath warm against Nicole's ear. "Remember when I told you there were other options for your music? This is what I was working on, hoping you'd be a part of it. Are you ready to do some music studio sessions with me?"

Nikki's heart soared. The thought of embarking on this creative journey with Michael, combining their talents and faith, filled her with an electrifying sense of purpose. Nicole nodded and squeezed his hand.

Michael raised a hand, and the congregation slowly quieted, their curiosity piqued. "That's just part of my news. Now, I'd like to share another blessing in my life."

With a deep breath, he released Nicole's
hand, his eyes never leaving hers as he
dropped to one knee. The room collectively
held its breath as he opened a deep red velvet
box, revealing a sparkling diamond ring that
caught the light and shimmered like their
shared dreams. "Nicole McClellan, I have
loved you for a long time and I promise to love
you for all our time to come. You were my first
love and I want you to be my long-lasting love.
You fill me with inspiration and joy. I want what
was once our 'Dreamland' in song to become
our reality. Would you do me the honor of
becoming my wife?"

Tears welled up in Nikki's eyes, her whole
being trembling with overwhelming joy. Her
voice quivered as she nodded emphatically.
"Yes, definitely yes."

Michael's hands shook slightly as he
slipped the ring onto her finger, sealing their
promise. He rose to his feet and gently kissed

her cheek, then wrapped his arm around her shoulder with a sense of pride and fulfillment. "Everyone, I'd like to introduce you to the future Mrs. Nicole Wilkerson."

The congregation stood in unison, applause filling the room like a symphony. Nikki felt her heart swell to bursting with a happiness she had never imagined possible. This moment, this perfect moment, would forever remind her that love was more profound than fame and could fill her life with a joy that no stage ever could.

The end but the beginning of a lifetime of love and music together!

Thank you for taking the time to read this book. Would you do me a favor and leave a review on wherever you purchased the book? I would greatly appreciate it and this will help other readers discover this book.

***

Why I created a character

who had an alcohol addiction

On a global scale, Alcohol Use Disorder (AUD) has been the seventh-leading risk factor for premature death and disability. Alcohol misuse was the leading risk factor for death and disability among people ages 15 to 49.

Approximately 14.0% of total deaths among people ages 20 to 39 were alcohol attributable.(source: https://www.niaaa.nih.gov/alcohols-effectshealth/alcohol-topics/alcohol-facts-andstatistics/global-burden)

If you think you might have a problem with alcohol addiction or know somebody who does, here are some links for Alcoholics Anonymous that you might find helpful.

https://www.aa.org/what-is-aa

https://www.aa.org/twelve-steps-twelvetraditions

https://www.aa.org/aa-around-the-world

AUTHOR BIO AND BOOK LIST

Christine Henderson's short stories, poems, and inspirational pieces have been published in regional and national magazines and numerous anthologies about family life. Her recipes have also won awards. Other published works include sweet romance novels, children's picture books, devotionals, and a cookbook. Discover all her books and details on new releases at:
https://amzn.to/447yw09

Her blog features weekly interviews with bestselling authors who discuss their upcoming books and offer eBook giveaways. You can read it at
https://thewritechris.blogspot.com/

INSPIRATIONAL ROMANCE NOVELS

Finding Love at Christmas: 12 Heartwarming Christian Romance Novellas for the Holidays: This box set of sweet romances stories can be pre-ordered at a discount. Resale date is October 15, 2024. Her book takes place in Aspen and is called **Falling in Love Despite Christmas Miscalculations**

The Sweetest Delights in Life: Jasmine delights in making sweet treats. Trevor's a food critic who doesn't pull punches. There's a definite attraction when they meet. But will their differences be the right mix? Or will it be a love recipe doomed to fall as fast as a souffle?

PICTURE BOOKS FOR FAMILIES TO READ TOGETHER

A Special Digital Scrapbook Memory - Eek! Who wants to do homework? Not Angie! She's too busy creating an online scrapbook about all the fun her family had at the beach this summer. Can't she just ignore her homework - especially memorizing her Bible verses for class. But a chat with her mom changes her perspective with happy results.

Jesus Loves Me This Much! And Guess What? He loves you, too! Through captivating illustrations and engaging storytelling, children will come to understand that Jesus's love is always with them, no matter what they do or where they go. Spark meaningful conversations about faith and love as you share this enchanting story with your little ones.

'Twas the Day Before Christmas: Go past the hustle and bustle of the holidays with a group of carolers whose singing spreads cheer and touches the hearts of those who listen. The tale is told in the poetic style of Clement Moore's writing, but this focus is on the first Christmas. You'll want to make reading this book a yearly tradition.

DEVOTIONALS

The First Noel–Digging Deeper into Christ's Birth – Come delve into Christ's birth story starting with the surprising announcement to Mary that she would give birth to the Messiah. It concludes with the visit by the Magi who bring gifts for a King — or in this case, the King of Kings.

Each day begins with a scripture reading, shows an early hymn that highlights the scripture, adds notes on the reading, discussion questions to ponder, and provides links to historical details for further study. BUY THE BOOK & SUPPORT A CAUSE: All sale proceeds will go to a prison ministry.

Exploring the Bible: Prayers, Poems, Praises, Bible Verses and Fun Pages – *5-Star Reader's Favorite Rating*. This book provides 15 lessons to engage the young reader. Each includes Bible verses to remember, poems, gratitude pages, and Bible related games, puzzles, & coloring pages.

A Closer Walk with Jesus: 52-Week Prayer Journal for Women
Transform your daily prayer life with this beautiful and inspiring women's prayer journal. Designed with the busy woman in mind, this 52week journal provides a simple and organized way to deepen your relationship with God. Each week offers inspiring Bible verses, thoughtful prompts, space for reflection, and a guided section for writing out your thoughts.

COOKBOOK

Let's Share a Meal: Comfort Food For Family & Friends. Come join me on my food journey as I share favorite recipes I've made over the years as well as those shared with me from family and friends. Though I consider myself a "foodie," these recipe ingredients can be found in most markets. The directions don't require fancy kitchen tools to make.